# Need to Know

A Grayson Cole Thriller

By

Sean Smith

**Other Books by Sean Smith**

Unleashing Colter's Hell ~ 2012

Lost Cause ~ 2014

**Praise for Unleashing Colter's Hell**

"Buy this book." Ranger Magazine

2013 Reader's Favorite Gold Medal

"This thriller is not only a superb novel of suspense, but it will remain with you as one of the scariest books you will ever read. Don't be surprised to see "Unleashing Colter's Hell" making it to the Top Ten Bestseller's list." Lee Ashford for Readers' Favorite

"A Great Novel." Amazon Reader Review

Need to Know

I would like to acknowledge the following people for their support and assistance in the writing of this novel. Mark Ostersmith, Marlla Moohn, Christi and Gil Smith, my wife and kids, and all my fans.

*It's easier to fool people than to convince them they have been fooled.*

Mark Twain

*I occasionally think how quickly our differences, worldwide, would vanish if we were facing an alien threat from outside this world.*

Ronald Reagan in a speech with President Mikhail Gorbachev, 1988

## Prologue

## Airspace outside Mount Rainier National Park, June 24, 1947

Kenneth Arnold was the 32-year-old founder of the Great Western Fire Control Company. Born in Minnesota, he grew up in Western Montana and was the chief executive of a fire suppression business. This job required frequent travel including many trips throughout the Pacific Northwest.

Arnold decided that getting his pilot's license would ease the stress of travel. He bought one of the 16 Model A2 aircraft built by Callair for civilian flight. The A2 was a low-wing, two-seater craft. It had a single Avco Lycoming O-290-a engine creating 125hp. That horsepower produced a top speed of 140 mph and a range of approximately 350 miles. Its operating ceiling was just under 16,000 feet.

That ceiling wouldn't matter today as Arnold piloted his plane from Chehalis, Washington to Yakima. He'd departed Chehalis at 2:15pm and was over the tiny western Washington mining town of Mineral about 45 minutes later.

The day was exceptionally clear, with more than 150 miles of visibility in every direction. The towering 14,410-foot, snowcapped Mount Rainier was off to his left. Mount St. Helens, the Fuji-like young volcano, was off his right shoulder. The equally impressive and broad Mount Adams was ahead and to his right. Way off in the distance to his left was Mount Baker, which sat astride the United States/Canadian border. The mountains reminded Arnold of giant scoops of ice cream, as if some super giant had walked from Oregon to Canada dropping enormous sundaes every 50 miles. *Truly beautiful.*

Arnold banked his plane slightly to the left until his compass read 45 degrees. The change in course would add a few extra minutes to his flight to the farming community of Yakima. But the extra time was worth it. The Army was offering $5,000 reward to anyone who located the wreckage of a

U.S. Marine Corps C-46 transport that had crashed on the slopes of Mount Rainier six months before.

The Marine transport plane had been one of six planes heading from San Diego to Seattle, ferrying more than 200 Marines. The pilots were flying on instruments at roughly 9,000 feet. The weather was bad that December day, forcing four planes to turn back.  Two pushed on, one making it eventually to Seattle. The other was blown badly off course and never made it to its final destination.  The military believes the plane flew into the Tahoma glacier on Mount Rainier's western slope.  A military search had failed to locate the plane.  Thus, the reward.

Arnold slowed his airspeed slightly by pulling back on the throttle. If he was to spot the wreckage, speed wasn't necessary.  He'd need to maximize his time over the suspected crash site.

The Tahoma glacier was a massive river of slow-flowing ice. It covered nearly a quarter of the volcano's west side. It was an enormous area to search.  *No wonder the military hadn't found the downed plane*, Arnold thought, as he began his scan of the winter wonderland below.

He'd only been searching for about 15 minutes but began to think the effort fruitless,  but on the off-chance that he would spot something, he pushed on. A few more minutes of searching and Arnold concluded it was hopeless. He began a slow right-hand turn back to his original course, when a bright flashing light off to his left caught his eye.

"What the hell?" Arnold said aloud. The flashing light reminded him of sunbeams bouncing off a mirror. *Odd* he thought. He ended his turn and brought his wings to level flight in order to get a better view.

Prior to leaving Chehalis, Arnold filed a flight plan before takeoff and been told by air traffic control that the skies would be nearly empty on his trip. The few planes that he was alerted to would be coming from the south, not the north.

Yet, there was the flashing object or, on second look, objects: *One, two, three* Arnold counted to himself. On closer inspection, he concluded there were nine maybe ten distinctive objects closing from the north. It was hard to tell. The flashing made it hard to count, but he finally settled on nine.

*Those have to be reflections*, Arnold concluded. *The sun is playing tricks on me.* He took off his sunglasses. Perhaps they were causing the effect. Nope, the lights were still there. Maybe his plane's windows were at fault. The pilot rolled his plane back and forth, but the objects remained in their current positions. The plane's movement had no impact upon the flashing lights. No, the flashing lights were coming from real objects.

*What's going on?* Arnold could see that the craft were going to pass directly in front of him so he pushed his throttle forward. The engine revved, increasing its RPM and airspeed. *Perhaps I can get close enough to see what these craft are.*

Arnold continued to track the lights. Yes, there clearly were nine distinct objects. They flew almost in a straight line. *Birds wouldn't do that. A new type of plane perhaps? My God, they are moving fast.*

Arnold checked his watch. He'd first seen the lights over Mount Baker just 5 minutes and 17 second before. Now they were racing in front of Mount Rainier. *That's more than 150 miles in a little more than 300 seconds.* He did a quick calculation in his head and came to the startling speed of 1,700 mph! T*hat can't be right! America doesn't have anything that could move that fast.*

Arnold had read World War II reports on the Americans' capture of Nazi technology, including jet airplanes. But everything he'd read indicated these planes could at best reach 650 mph. These craft were obviously going nearly three times that speed!

Arnold pushed his craft up to its maximum. He wanted to get closer. The flashing objects were passing right in front of him now.

Arnold could easily make out their shape now. They were dark, incredibly thin, crescent shaped objects. When viewed from the side, they seemed to disappear.

The objects broke formation and began erratically flying around Mount Rainier's central peak. The jerking flight path reminded Arnold of the movement of a startled cat. First in one place, then another, then still another. *That's impossible!* But there it was. The objects were jumping all over the place. It appeared they were looking for something on the mountain,  just as he was.  *This can't be happening.*

But like Arnold, the objects eventually gave up their search and reformed a straight line formation and headed at supersonic speed toward Mount Adams some 50 miles to the southeast. Arnold watched them pass the second volcano and disappear from view.

He pulled back on his throttle, slowing his craft to its normal cruising speed. He checked his watch again. *I must be going crazy*, he considered. The entire episode lasted less than 7 minutes.

**Mount Rainier National Park, WA Friday, May 4ᵗʰ, Present Year, Early Morning**

"From National Public Radio in Washington D.C., I'm Ira Stone," the radio on Grayson Cole's Park Service issued SUV sang out. "It's six a.m. here is the news."

Cole adjusted the volume, turning it up to overcome the whir of the SUV's tires on the park blacktop.

"In international news, treaty talks between the United States and the Russian Federation on nuclear arms reduction broke down yesterday over something as simple as the counting of bombs," NPR's Scott Mickens stated from his Switzerland location.

*"The counting of bombs?"* Cole fumed. *"Are you kidding me? The world might hang in the balance and our diplomats are arguing over how to count."*

The road ahead took a wide turn around a pair of centuries old Douglas fir trees. The radio signal faltered as the public radio station's signal was blocked momentarily. Cole didn't bother adjusting the station or volume this time. He knew the signal problem wasn't due to any technical difficulty at the Seattle NPR station or electronic problems with his vehicle's radio. Rather, the signal's fade was more likely due to the 14,000ft volcano just coming into view on his left side.

Mount Rainier was a snow capped volcano that climbed nearly 3 miles into the Washington sky. British explorer George Vancouver had been the first European to spot the mountain and named it after his friend and fellow explorer Peter Rainier. The local Indians referred to the stratovolcano as Tahoma or the "mother of waters." Rainier's profile was made all the more impressive in that it towered thousands of feet over the foothills that clustered around its base. So large was the mountain that, on clear days, its summit could be seen hundreds of miles away in Eastern Washington.

Mount Rainier was the most prominent natural feature in Washington State. Its image adorned just about everything in the Northwest including vehicle license plates, U.S. quarters, and postage stamps. So, dominate was Mount Rainier's impact upon people of the northwest that locals could tell the weather by merely asking one another if the Mountain was out.

The static coming out of Cole's radio got worse and broke the ranger's contemplation of the mountain, yet snatches of dialogue continued to break through.

"The President is not optimistic . . . tension high . . . doomsday clock moved to three minutes of midnight," broke through the static.

Cole piloted his vehicle around another bend, the radio signal improved dramatically as the mountain obviously no longer served as a massive block between his vehicle and the Seattle radio station. The announcer went on. "Talks have broken down over the counting of militarily useful warheads. Specifically, the United States wants the definition of useful warheads to include what military experts view as currently obsolete, but could be made functional with modifications. The Russians oppose the broader definition. The two countries view on what constitutes a useful warhead is driven by their current stockpiles. The US over the last several years had spent time and energy on upgrading and modernizing their warheads, while decommissioning their older weapons. Meanwhile, the Russians have fewer modernized warheads but a larger stockpile of older weapons. In a nutshell, if one counts the older weapons it will be the Russian stockpile that takes a big hit. If one excludes them, it's the U.S."

Cole's SUV came around a corner and into a forest clearing. Mount Rainier came into full view with the first hints of sunlight painting its highest reaches. It didn't matter how many times Cole drove this road, he was always struck by this first view of the mountain.

Rainier's present volcanic cone was relatively young, only about 500,000 years old, and still active. It's last eruption was sometime in the 1800s.

Cole was struck by the beauty of the mountain. The combination of snow and ice, mixed with blue gray rock made for an awe inspiring sight. Cole had to agree with John Muir who, in 1893, recognized that Rainier should be protected for future generations. In 1899 Congress would designate the peak a national park, one of only four sites enjoying that title at the time.

Cole's vehicle passed through the clearing and back into the dense forest of firs, cedars, and alders that skirted the lower reaches of the mountain.

The radio announcer's drone again broke Cole's contemplation. "Military experts and diplomats aren't optimistic the impasse with be breached anytime soon. Tension between the two super powers has not been this high since the cold war, with both militaries going on a heightened state of alert. Talks continue on . . ."

Cole snapped off the radio. He'd had enough of politics. *"My God,"* he thought. *"Humanity might destroy itself over what is considered a useful weapon."*

The mountain came back into view, filling the SUV's entire windshield. The mountain was massive. So large in fact, one couldn't really appreciate its size unless one was on it.

Like its sister Cascade volcanos, Rainier was what experts referred to as a stratovolcano. Stratovolcanoes tended to produce more explosive and violent eruptions than their Hawaiian shield volcano counterparts.

Cole's SUV continued to ascend the mountain's winding roads. Higher and higher he climbed passing 4,000 ft. above sea level. The forests that served as the volcano's skirt started to thin and ultimately disappear as Cole passed into the park's alpine zone. Here the small, thin, and scrawny Alpine fir dominated the landscape. Yet, despite the sickly appearance of many of these trees, many were decades and even centuries old. The harsh alpine climate took its toll on the trees' appearance, but they evolved in such conditions and even thrived.

Rounding a final turn and breaking out of a last stand of hardy fir, the Park's Jackson visitor center came into view. A new center built to replace the previous 1960's era visitor center, was an iconic A frame structure. Large picture windows in the back of the building gave visitors, on a clear day, an unobstructed view of the volcano. Something the old building could not match.

The visitor center's parking lot was sparsely dotted with cars, trucks and a few campers this morning. Cole wasn't surprise. It was still early in the season.

The real crush of visitors wouldn't arrive for several more weeks. Beyond the parking lot was the Paradise Inn Hotel. A turn of the last century park lodge, that rivaled those found in bigger parks like Yellowstone and Yosemite. It's log and timber construction, reminded Cole of something out of Switzerland or Austria. America had done something right when it built these hotels. Today's new park accommodations, if they are built at all, are more often constructed for economic reasons rather than aesthetic ones. The West Thumb Motor Inn at Yellowstone immediately came to mind. Remembering that typical roadside motel triggered a shudder through Cole's body. The growing mountain off to his left, quickly made him forget the matchbox like Motor Inn.

Although, Cole would have enjoyed spending the day in Paradise Lodge's cavernous lobby, drinking hot chocolate and talking with visitors about their park adventures, that wasn't his final destination. Rather, he turned off the park's main road and pulled into the parking lot of a smaller A frame building. The smaller building's parking lot was recently plowed of the several inches of snow that had fallen overnight. The snow constituted little more than a dusting up here at over 5,000ft, but it was enough to keep down the crowds. Few wanted to venture up to Mount Rainier when there was even a threat of snow. Unfortunately, a fair number of park visitors had lost their lives believing a slight snowfall wouldn't harm them. Blinding whiteout blizzards could come up at almost any time, threatening anyone unfortunate enough to be out in the storm.

But that wasn't the case this morning. The previous evening's snowstorm had passed. The cobalt blue sky was clear, with only a few scattered clouds off to the East. They could spell trouble Cole thought. Just to be safe he'd get the latest weather report before heading out.

Cole had been Mount Rainier Superintendent for a little more than six months. After his detail back east, he'd barely had time to return to his trailer in Yellowstone to pick up his few belongings say goodbye to old friends, and get his dog before it was time to report for his new assignment.

His previous park service assignments had prepared him for the rigors of his new job, but just barely. His days used to be spent chasing down bad guys, fighting fires, assisting with search and rescues, restoring wildlife and helping the occasional wayward visitor. Now his days were dominated by countless budget meetings, personnel reviews, public hearings, and weekly conference calls. He seldom actually got out into the field anymore. When he had the opportunity to get out into the park, he guarded it like it was manna from Heaven. In one sense it was. Cole drew inspiration for his work by actually getting out into the parks and interacting with the visitors and park resources. A walk through the woods, even a short one, could do wonders to recharge his batteries. He wasn't going to miss his climb today no matter what.

He parked the SUV in one of the "Park Service Only" parking spaces, turned off the engine and set the parking brake. He exited the vehicle and walked toward the building's door. Printed in fading gold letters a sign hung on the door "Ranger Station, Climbing Division." Cole opened the door. A small bell rang behind the visitor desk, alerting the ranger on duty that someone was coming in.

Every visitor that wanted to climb the mountain, which numbered thousands every year, had to obtain a permit. A few misguided visitors balked at this requirement. "Why do I need a permit to climb a mountain the public owns?" they asked. Cole had heard variations of this question at other parks where he'd worked. The answer may vary based on the location, but it was generally the same. Permits were required to climb or camp or boat to protect park resources and wildlife as well as visitors. Many park visitors' lives were saved by the information contained on their permits.

He walked up to the visitor desk. A young female climbing ranger was standing behind the counter ready to assist the new boss.

Cole had met her once before, during his new employee orientation. *"Becky, Betty, Beth? What was her name?"* he thought as he approached the desk. *"Beth. Yes, that was it."*

"Good morning Beth," Cole said reaching the desk.

"Good morning sir," the young ranger replied. "You headed up the mountain this morning?"

"The Mountain," was what locals called Mount Rainier. Ask anyone within a hundred miles of this volcano if the mountain was out today, and they would immediately know the question referred to Rainier and was a question about the weather. Was the mountain out; meant was the weather clear enough to see the volcano's summit? If the answer was yes, it was likely to be a great day. The answer was clearly yes today.

"Yes, as a matter of fact I am. Looking to hike up to Camp Muir today and even possibly spend the night," Cole explained. "That is if there is room up there."

"Plenty," Beth answered. "No one is up there." She turned to her computer and punched a couple buttons on the keyboard. "In fact, no one is scheduled to be up there all weekend. It looks like you will have the chalet all to yourself."

Camp Muir was a stone hut built in 1921 to serve as a base camp for climbers going onto the summit. For those not making the last push to the top, it served as a great location for camping and taking in the view.

"Good to know," Cole had hoped that would be the case. He'd barely had a minute to himself since he arrived at the park. A weekend of isolation would do wonders for his mental health.

"There's food and water up there to last a week. As well as firewood," Beth continued.

"Perfect." Cole agreed. "Would you hand me one of the climbing radios?"

Beth handed Cole a Motorola UHF two way radio and blank climbing permit. The Superintendent checked the radio's charge and adjusted its squelch. All appeared in order and he clipped the walkie talkie to his belt. He next proceeded to fill out the permit paperwork. He needed to make everything legal. God forbid one of the park's critics find out the Superintendent had been given special treatment. It would take weeks of PR busy work to clean up that mess.

"Sir," Beth went on. "I thought you'd like to see the weather report for the next few days." The young ranger pushed a computer printout of the five day forecast from weather.com across the visitor center desk. Cole glanced at the outlook while continuing to fill out his permit. All looked good, at least from a weather stand point.

> Temperatures in the 50 to 60s
> at Paradise.  Clear skies for the
> next two to three days, with a
> 10 percent chance of snow fall
> on Monday.

"We also have reports of avalanche and rock slides on Ingraham Glacier above Disappointment Cleaver," Beth said matter of fact, "but this shouldn't be a concern if you don't venture past Camp Muir."

Cole didn't intend to go beyond Muir.  Traveling beyond the base camp required what's called a technical climb.  The trail after Muir and eventually to the summit traversed ice fields, cornice overhangs, and basalt outcroppings littered with house sized boulders. Any of these obstacles could cause one to lose his footing and cast a poor climber tumbling down the mountain for thousands of feet. Glaciers were even scarier, as their dangers such as hundreds of feet deep crevasses could be hidden by paper thin snow bridges.  One step onto these snow veils could send the hapless climber falling into a hole more than a football field deep. There would be no way to recover the body or anything else that was unfortunate enough to fall into one of those fissures. Most people, at least the smart ones, who ventured beyond Muir went with a team. A team that was roped together and could help prevent tragedy. Or, in the case disaster struck, rescue each other.

Even with the best equipment, training, and teammates, climbers still died on Mount Rainier. Nearly every year someone was killed making the ascent. On good years, the death toll was less than half a dozen. On bad years, whole strings of climbers were wiped out in a single avalanche, and no amount of training or preparation could prevent it. If the mountain didn't want someone to climb it, it could kill with as little effort as it would take an elephant to snuff out an ant.

Cole contemplated this fact as he continued to fill out the climbing permit. He was grateful he wouldn't be going beyond Camp Muir on this trip. He'd climb to the summit at some point. It was an unwritten requirement for every Superintendent to make the assent at least once, if not several times. But today wasn't the day, if for no other reason than he had no one else going on this trip. There would be no one to help him if he got into trouble.

He paused for a second when reaching the form's section that asked for a home phone. Cole had only recently moved into a house. He'd been living in temporary park accommodations these past few months while he'd looked for a permanent dwelling. He'd found a small house in nearby Eatonville. It was a two bedroom 1950's era house. It was nothing fancy, but had a garage and small back yard for his dog. It was a place to hang his hat. He'd only just gotten his phone hooked up last week and still hadn't committed the number to memory.

He stared off into space trying to conjure up the number from the ether. His eyes spotted a visitor information panel hanging on the wall behind the information desk. The top on the panel read:

**"Why are Mount Rainier's glaciers receding?"**

"That's new isn't it?" Cole said pointing at the panel.

"Yes it is," Beth replied. "It just went up yesterday." Beth went on, anticipating Cole's next question. "We've been getting a number of visitor and climbing questions about the impact melting glaciers have on climbing routes and other things."

"Hmm," Cole muttered.

"Most interesting," Beth was enjoying the opportunity to educate her boss, "is the fact that as these glaciers melt, they eject or reveal things that have been buried in the ice for years."

"Really?"

"Yes, all kinds of stuff.  Mostly rocks and old trees, Native American artifacts, junk left by previous climbers, and an occasional dead animal turn up at the glacier's boundary."

Cole scribbled his signature across the bottom of the permit, making his paperwork all official.

"Would you mind doing us a favor?" Beth asked.

"I suppose," Cole said sliding his paperwork across the information desk toward Beth.

"We need to refill camp Muir's climbing cache. Would you mind taking up some ropes, harnesses, and other climbing equipment?"

Beth pointed to a green canvas, army issued duffle bag stored in the room's corner. It didn't look too heavy to Cole and likely wouldn't take too much effort to haul up to Muir. Besides, Cole wanted to be seen by his staff as one of the Rangers. He wanted to be seen as someone who pulled his weight, not just a desk jockey like too many Superintendents in the service now days.

Cole grabbed the bag and opened it on the visitor center desk. As expected, it contained climbing rope, crampons, a couple of helmets, head lamps, and boot gators. A couple harnesses and a rescue sling were also included.

"Those are new crampons," Beth explained pointing at a pair of metal plates with spikes.

Cole picked up a pair and examined them more closely. Crampons were made to be affixed to climbing boots with elastic bands, improving a climber's ability to cross snow and ice fields.

*"They look like some type of cleats medieval Knights might wear,"* Cole noted turning the spikes over in his hands. He eventually placed them back in the duffle bag.

The bag was heavier than he'd anticipated but he couldn't balk at carrying up the gear now. Besides, the equipment was needed at Muir and Cole was going up, so it made sense for him to carry it.

He repacked the remaining equipment in the bag, and gave a slight salute to Beth. The young ranger took Cole's permit, dated it with an ink stamp and handed Cole his copy. "You're all official now sir!" she said with a smile. "Enjoy your stay at Camp Muir."

"Will do. If all goes well, you won't see me until Monday." Cole replied with a wave of his hand. He grabbed the bag, flung it over his shoulder and headed toward the door.

## Above Camp Muir, Friday May 4th, Early Morning

Aimee Crocker could see the sun clearly above the horizon. Washington's eastern frontier was awash in reds, oranges, and even some pink and purple. It was a beautiful site. And the 30 something Midwesterner would have loved to spend all morning taking in the view, but she couldn't. She had important work today, life changing, no world changing work.

The climb to camp Muir had been harder than she imagined. Crocker was in good shape, running half marathons often, doing yoga, and eating a balanced diet. To the average person, Crocker was what most aspired to be. But one thing her Midwest training hadn't and really couldn't prepare her for was what Mount Rainier had in spades, elevation. From its base to camp Muir was a 5,000ft climb, which by itself wasn't all that troubling, but Mount Rainier's base starts at nearly 5,000ft above sea level. So her climb to Camp Muir meant she was nearly two miles above her normal elevation.

Ten thousand feet was serious elevation, it was nearly as high as the flight level where the FAA required pilots to use oxygen if flying in an unpressurized plane. Crocker logically knew the air was thin, she'd done her homework before making the climb. Logic and understanding could only take one so far, she was

27

also physically feeling the elevation. Her breath was deep and rhythmic, with significant effort put into each exhale. The "pressure breathing" was a necessary routine to fully empty her lungs, allowing her to gulp in a larger volume of the oxygen poor air. Without this practice, she'd be oxygen deprived and susceptible to collapse.

Crocker was climbing with two other men, who followed an equally labored breathing method. The three's rhythmic whew, whew, whew of their breaths reminded Crocker of the chug, chug, chug of a steam powered train engine. It was nearly hypnotic and helped her keep her mind on the mission at hand.

Crocker had grown up in the Midwest, or more correctly settled in the Midwest, Nebraska to be precise. Growing up, "where are you from?" had been one of the hardest questions for Crocker to answer and often produced a "how long do you have?" response. Crocker's father and mother had been in the Army. Army life was at best predictable for one thing, near regular redeployments. Nearly every two years, like clockwork, Crocker's parents would get a new assignment. Almost overnight, the family would pack up and ship off for the new base, often hundreds of miles and several time zones from the previous one. Army life didn't afford the development of deep roots, but it did provide Crocker the opportunity to see much of the world. She followed her parents to bases in Washington State, Alaska, Germany, Japan and Saudi Arabia. The family's final stop was California's Fort Ord.

Crocker's father, Major Thomas Crocker was in Army intelligence. He'd been sent to Europe and Japan to spy on the Russians. In the Middle East it was Al Qaeda, the Taliban, and ISIS. It also seemed to Crocker that some aspect of her father's work would end up on TV or in the news, however Major Crocker was never attributed to it. That was to be expected.

That all changed when they moved to California. Her father and mother no longer worked in foreign intelligence. In fact, to Crocker it appeared her parents work and her understanding of it disappeared into a black hole. Her parents no longer talked of, or even in passing, referenced their work. In fact, their association with the Federal government and military appeared to end while they were stationed at Fort Ord. Crocker's father started to refer to himself as a consultant on advanced technologies for private corporations. This new work required him to be away on private business for weeks at a time, sometimes overseas. However, Crocker began to doubt these stories as her father, on more than one occasion, failed to take his passport when he was supposedly out of the country.

Crocker chocked this up to her parents still being in intelligence despite what they told her. It made the most sense that her parents' remained employed in some sort of cloak and dagger, why else live on base? But it troubled her that they no longer, even if in obscure reference, felt able to include their daughter.

The new routine continued like this for years, but it all changed when her father returned from what she believed had been a two week trip to London to review theoretically groundbreaking engine technology. Technology that had recently been captured from the Russians. Yet, it was obvious on his return that the trip had been anything but ordinary. His physical state decayed quickly after his return. His complexion grew ashen over a mere few weeks. His eyes appeared to sink back into his skull while he lost significant weight, slowly taking on the appearance of a skeleton. Even more troubling to Crocker, her always strong father suffered a series of mental breakdowns. His mood swung erratically from panic and anxiety to depression and sadness, often ending in uncontrollable sobbing.

Both Crocker and her mother were at a loss to explain the deterioration.

This went on for months, until almost as suddenly it all ended. It was as if a heavy load had been lifted from her father. His mood appeared lighter; his physical state also seemed to improve as her father obviously put on weight.

Crocker pressed her father on what had changed. Why the reversal? Rather than providing a straight answer, her father rather cryptically stated, "All will be known soon." Crocker guessed her father had come to some type of decision, some type of cross roads in his work. She speculated that the source of his downward spiral was work related, and that he was likely to move in a new direction. Maybe a new assignment she guessed. She hoped. Whatever it was, her father was better and things were once again looking up for her family.

Her father died shortly thereafter however. The military and the local police deemed it a one car accident. One car accident, Crocker quickly learned was a euphemism for suicide. The official report in graphic detail, laid out the accident. How her father's car had hit a tree at a high rate of speed. No skid marks or any other evidence were present indicating the driver had tried to avoid collision. No alcohol or drugs were found in his system. The conclusion being he'd been under no mind altering drugs. The final report made the case that her father had raced his car directly and deliberately into a tree. He'd been killed instantly in large part because he'd failed to wear a seat belt. His body was thrown several dozen feet from the vehicle and showed severe blunt force trauma to the head and torso. The coroner assured her mother that the good Major was killed instantly.

Crocker tried to accept this final report despite its troubling implications. She tried her best to move on with her life and to all outside appearances had done so. She had gone onto college at the University of Washington, getting her undergraduate degree in economics. She received a Master's of Public Policy from Stanford. After leaving Palo Alto she'd envisioned working in a policy think tank or perhaps as an economics professor at some university.

Crocker and her mother remained close over the years, but Crocker's need to get a job and become a self-sustaining adult meant she spent less and less time with her mom. Eventually, her mother's health also deteriorated and she passed a few years back. While Crocker couldn't prove it, she was convinced her mom had died of a broken heart, having lost her partner of more than 25 years.

Her mother's death had been a blow, but just as she suspected others did she came to accept it. People grow old and eventually die. That is life. However, despite her outward appearance, Crocker never fully shook her father's death. It haunted her, especially at night. She'd often be awoken by nightmares, her father muttering over and over, "All will be known soon."

A few months back, at the behest of her psychologist, she had decided to reexamine her father's death. The psychologists' thinking was that her subconscious was trying to tell her something. Some bit of foreign or alien information was breaking through to her rational mind. A reinvestigation might uncover that bit of troubling information, which kept her from moving on. Once uncovered the psychologist proposed, the two would attempt to remove the troubling information or like an oyster with an irritating bit of sand, coat it and in essence remove it as well. Either way, the process of reinvestigating her father's death, Crocker believed was the psychologist's way of helping her find closure or something as close to it as possible.

If that was the psychologists plan, it failed. Crocker was hesitant to revisit the reports and memos, but once she did she threw herself into the process. She quickly realized the official report was slip shod at best. Questions had been left unanswered. Information wasn't provided. It was as if the military wanted the matter to quickly and quietly go away. This didn't bother Crocker too much. She'd grown up in the military and had seen many "official" reports and investigations which to the civilian seemed shoddy. But this one was different, this one detailed the death of her father and he deserved better than what now was appearing to be a cut and paste report.

The more she reviewed the official report, the more she couldn't shake the feeling that something was amiss. She combed through every official bit of data in the report, from the vehicle mileage her father was driving to the clothes he was wearing. It was all there, yet, it was the description of her father's accident that struck her as most odd. The report defined a single car accident at milepost 76 on two lane State Route 706. The report's author noted the car had struck a "500 year old Douglas Fir tree at nearly 60 miles an hour."

Crocker sent the California Highway Patrol (CHP) an information request seeking additional information on the single car accident on State Route 706 dated October 17, 2010. She was shocked and frustrated when the CHP reply came back that "no such accident exists in our database."

*What the hell is going on?* Crocker remembered thinking. Several long and angry phone calls later, Crocker was convinced the CHP wasn't hiding anything. Rather it was the military.

The location of the accident had been listed as CA State Route 706. But her investigation had made one thing clear, no accident on CA State Route 706 had occurred in 2010, because California had no State Route 706.

Following up with the Army regarding the non-existent State Route 706 led nowhere. As far as the Army was concerned, the report says CA State Route 706, therefore the accident happened on CA State Route 706. Crocker quickly realized she was going to get no more meaningful information from the military.

Her failure to find her father's actual place of death had been surprisingly troubling. Not knowing where he'd died was a kick in the gut, one she hadn't expected. She knew where her father was buried. She'd seen his body before internment in the local military graveyard. But not knowing where he actually died opened up all kinds of troubling and scary possibilities.

*Had her father been truly killed in a car crash?* She wondered. Yet more terrifying she questioned if his death had actually been an accident? These questions drove her on, pushing her to get to the bottom of this secret.

But where to look? Crocker decided to change tactics. If she couldn't figure out where her father had been killed, perhaps she could figure out what he'd been doing in his last hours. This line of questioning, she thought, might lead to new answers.

She reexamined the military report. It contained a listing of everything found in the car including both personal effects and military equipment. The personal items had been returned to Crocker and her mother. She remembered they were the expected things, a wallet, car keys, a ball cap. Nothing out of the ordinary. The report also provided a listing of military equipment found in the vehicle. Unfortunately, the items were listed by serial and item numbers, no description was provided. Crocker was assured there was no nefarious intent behind this listing; rather it was likely used at the request of an unnamed equipment manager.

After some digging and calling in some favors, she was able to match the item numbers with actual descriptions. Her mouth fell open upon reading the list which seemed something someone would take to Hoth, the ice planet in Star Wars.

The list included: one cold weather survival suit, including a pair of size 11 climbing boots and crampons, one climbing helmet with flashlight, one ice axe, 75ft of high-strength repelling rope, night vision and infrared goggles, one metal detector, and last but not least one high sensitivity Geiger counter. *"What the hell?"* she thought.

She rechecked the equipment list. Her father's signature was clearly scribbled across the bottom of the manifest. He had checked this equipment out. *But why?* If her father had meant to kill himself, why would he take equipment that would prepare him to make an apparent assault on Ice Station Zebra? It made no sense. Another dead end it appeared.

The search was becoming frustrating. It appeared that she might never get the answers she sought, until one day she had a chance encounter with her postal worker. It appeared an important letter had been misdirected up north. It was an expected Army response to one of her requests for information. After waiting several weeks for a letter that should have only taken days to deliver, she was suspicious when the postal service reported they had found it. "How could a letter meant for Monterrey end up in a town called Metaline. According to the postal worker it was a simple substitution error. The sender instead of typing CA for California in the address had entered WA which meant Washington. The letter was sent north in search of the non-existent address and bounced around the dead letter process, until finally being sent back to the Army.

When she finally received the nomad letter she could plainly see that the address had been entered incorrectly. The error was simply fixed by scratching out WA and replacing it with CA. After that, the letter had no problem finding her mailbox.

On seeing this mistake, Crocker wondered if something similar had happened in her father's fatality report. What if he hadn't been killed on California's State Route 706 but Washington's? The thought that she might be back on the right path filled her with a rush of excitement.

Crocker entered the new information into the google search engine, hit return, and presto. There it was. Washington State Route 706 Milepost 76 clearly indicated on google maps. But rather than bringing clarity, bringing closure to her father's death, the location of his crash brought more questions. The google map flag blinked on her screen, clearly within the boundary of Mount Rainier national park.

Additional google searches revealed that Mount Rainier was one of America's most iconic and surprisingly oldest national parks. The railroads had donated land, including the mountain's summit to the federal government to facilitate the establishment of the park. The park itself was approximately the 250,000 acres or roughly 3 times the size of Seattle, the nearby metropolis.

Yet, none of these facts were of interest to Crocker, rather it was the fact that Mount Rainier was a volcano that held her attention. Mount Rainier was a 14,000ft stratovolcano, one of the largest in the continental United States. According to the United States Geological Society, it was deemed one of the world's 10 most deadly volcanos.

"Why would her father kill himself, and more importantly why would he kill himself at Rainier?" she wondered. Crocker then remembered the cold winter survival gear in her father's car at the time of his death. *"What if he hadn't gone to die at Mount Rainier, but to climb the mountain instead?"*

That spark of insight got her thinking about her father's last words to her, "all would be revealed soon, I will soon return from the Looking Glass." *Could her father have been trying to tell her something before he left? What did he mean by all would be revealed? Where or what was the looking glass?*

More research revealed that "Through the Looking Glass and what Alice Found There" was the name of a Lewis Carroll novel better known today as Alice in Wonderland. *Curious and curiouser.*

Crocker pressed on in her research. There were pages and pages of information on the novel, its meaning, and impact upon society. Crocker was surprised to learn her father was such an Alice in Wonderland fan. But it made some strange sense. Her father dealt in secrets, shadow worlds, places and situations which on first glance appeared one way, yet on closer inspection were something entirely different.

Thus was the life of a spy or counter intelligence agent. The thought of her father during his military

39

days brought to mind an image of him in his Army uniform, a flag patch on his right shoulder, a sleeve insignia patch with the Latin term "Nihil est enim, ut Videtur." Nothing is as it Seems, on his left. Thinking back on it, Crocker always thought the patch odd. Nothing is as it seems? *What could that mean?* she asked herself.

Another quick google search of the patch, turned up a YouTube video of a former British member of parliament (MP) turned UFO investigator. A UFOLOGIST as they were called in the UFO community, Crocker came to learn.

The former minister was an average looking man, middle aged with a receding tuft of uncombed black hair. He was of average build and his appearance likely didn't leave a lasting impression on people. However, his choice of topics and his passion for his subject clearly did.

The audience sat in rapt wonder as the former MP detailed his personal experience with alien lifeforms including his abduction as a child. He explained his first contact had taken place when he was a mere six years old and continued to today. Crocker knew that many people believed and claimed they had been visited and abducted by aliens. However, this man was different in that besides personal information, he also claimed professional knowledge of their existence. He asserted his work as a public official had provided privileged access to secret government reports and files on the alien matter.

If her father's "return from the Looking Glass" promise was the doorstep of the Alice in Wonderland rabbit hole, the British minister's speech was the descent into its deepest recesses. Crocker was aware of the UFO craze and how seriously some took the supposed phenomenon. But the British minister took understanding of the UFO culture to a whole new level. For one, he claimed that the earth was a way station, gathering point, or strategic base for alien beings, and that it had been such for millennia if not from the beginning of time. The minister claimed that alien influences had been part of if not responsible for all human evolution. Crocker was immediately reminded of the scene in Stanley Kubrick's 2001 where an alien monolith, an advanced technology, sparked human imagination leading to jumps in understanding and advancement, until modern day.

The minister claimed the number one question he received from the public was "What do the aliens want?" He stated this question missed the mark, implying that there wasn't a single alien race with one agenda. Rather, he claimed with a straight face, "We know there are numerous alien races, at least six, all with designs on the earth. Some are benign and wish us no ill will, while others are actively working to our peril." Crocker chuckled out loud at such certainty. The 90 minute speech before a crowd of like-minded individuals provided many such statements, but little if any evidence to back up its main contentions that aliens were among us and they had designs on the third rock from the Sun. Crocker was about to close out the video, but stopped when the speaker turned to the United States' history with alien civilizations.

"The United States has known for decades, if not a century about the alien menace," the minister began. "It's government files, especially after World War II are filled with accounts of alien investigations, incidents, and cover ups. Most everyone knows about the famous UFO crash in Roswell New Mexico. What most don't realize is that the story was originally reported as a crashed UFO, replete with the recovery of occupants "obviously not of this world." It wasn't until after the Army came in that the official story changed from a crashed UFO to it being a downed weather balloon that landed in the New Mexico desert."

The speaker went on to claim that similar crashes and recoveries had taken place across the United States and the world. Also, that alien beings had been captured at several crash sites and were being held at various military bases around the country. The minister even claimed that Richard Nixon, on one trip to South Florida, had taken comedian Jackie Gleason, of all people, to the now abandoned Homestead Airforce base and shown the "Honeymooners" star the decomposing body of a reptilian like alien. According to the minister "Jack was visibly shaken by what he saw."

The minister turned his discussion to a secret American government agency, sparking Crocker's attention. He projected a picture on to his screen of a military patch, the patch her father had worn on his uniform. He described in great detail the purpose of the unit, which had been investigating UFO crashes all over the world. The minister claimed that the United States' and a few of its allies had known of alien life since just after the end of World War II. Most shocking however, was the minister's first hand claim, that the United States' was working with these aliens for purposes that were restricted to only those who "Need to Know." It was the most secret program in the country, with only a handful of people knowing of its existence and mission. It was so secret even American presidents were considered outside the loop of those who needed to know of its operations.

The minister shuffled his notes, pushed a button on his laptop and went on to detail one of the most controversial investigations, one that took place at Mount Rainier National Park. That really got

Crocker's attention. She turned up the volume and moved closer to her computer screen.

The minister claimed the mission was shrouded in secrecy and information requests on the matter turned up nothing. But his sources both inside the American and British government, assured him the Mount Rainier mission was of upmost priority at the time. However, the minister was convinced it had been a failure and pointed to a 1983 news report about an Air Force plane crash. The local news reported the crash as a tragic end to a routine training mission, but the minister's sources assured him it had been anything but routine. The four men who died when their C1 plane slammed into Mount Rainier's Success Glacier hadn't been on a training mission. Rather they were there on a top secret mission to recover an object that had crashed on the mountain's slopes more than three decades before.

All this information made Crocker's head spin. It couldn't be coincidence that her father had been part of this supposed super-secret agency and died in a single car accident with a trunk full of climbing gear at the same national park where more than a quarter century before four men from the same agency had died in a plane crash. Her father was clearly looking for something. And if her hunch was right, he was looking for the same thing the downed crew was searching for in 1983.

44

Crocker stopped for a moment to catch her breath.
Her climbing team was now well beyond Camp Muir,
Mount Rainier's 10,000 climbers' camp. She reached
to her belt and pulled out the attached REI water
bottle. Unscrewing the cap, she brought the bottle to
her lips to take a drink, but nothing came out. The
water was frozen solid. Crocker was surprised by this.
It was cold on the Mountain, but it didn't seem that
cold. In fact, Crocker felt it quite balmy and
contemplated removing one of the layers of clothes
she wore to release some of the body heat she was
generating. Yet her water bottle didn't lie. The water
was frozen. It was a stark reminder of how
inhospitable this mountain was even when weather
conditions were considered favorable. She'd hate to
be on this mountain if things got bad.

Her two climbing partners noticed Crocker had
stopped. They too paused. The sun was coming up in
the East now, but Crocker remained in the shadows.
She could see Mount Rainier's massive shadow
stretch out for miles from the summit. She'd be in the
dark for a couple of hours, until the sun finally
cleared the summit

Crocker hated climbing in the dark, especially on her
first real mountain climb. But her guides assured her
this was necessary. The snow and ice they were
climbing would become soft and weak in the morning
sun. Soft ice was deadly ice, as even the slightest

disturbance could bring thousands of tons of the material roaring down wiping anything or anyone unfortunate to be in its path completely off the mountain. She shuddered to think what it would be like to be overwhelmed by a wall of snow, ice and rock. Thus the team needed to get up, retrieve the object and be off the mountain as quickly as possible. At least that was the plan.

Crocker put the cap back on her water bottle. But instead of reapplying it to her belt, she tucked it inside her coat. Perhaps she could put her body heat to good use and melt her frozen drinking water. She zipped up her coat, and reached for her ice ax. She was about to signal to her team it was time to go when something caught her eye. A faint glint of sunlight reflected off something just above their current position.

Crocker retrieved a pair of binoculars from her backpack and zoomed in on the spot in question. On the ridgeline, roughly a couple thousand yards above her position, a black, triangle shaped object could be seen protruding out of the snowfield. Crocker thought it resembled something like a witch's hat, however the hat's point was rounded. She estimated the object was likely 3 to 4 meters tall, yet zooming into the surrounding snowbank, she guessed a significant portion of the object remained hidden from view. A rush of adrenaline shot through her body. *Could she*

*have found what she was looking for? Was this the
key to understanding why her father died on the
slopes of this mountain so many years ago?* She
wondered.

"Only one way to find out," she whispered to herself.
She replaced the binoculars in her pack. She slung the
pack over her shoulders, and cinched up the belt.
"That's where we're headed," she said pointing at the
far ridge.

## Below Camp Muir, Friday May 4th, Late Morning

Grayson Cole could see Camp Muir in the distance. His climb to Mount Rainier's eastern base camp was almost complete. He'd been climbing since 6:30 a.m. having made steady progress. He wasn't on a breakneck pace; it was obvious he wasn't going to get a medal for quickest ascent of the mountain. But that wasn't the point, at least not today. No this climb was about getting away from it all, about recharging his batteries, and reconnecting to why he'd joined the park service in the first place. For Cole the national park system was much more than pretty places or dusty old buildings. Rather, the parks held the key to understanding the country's past and promised hope for the future. Getting deep into a park's backcountry was the best way Cole found to reconnect to the park's promise. He'd also had this experience while standing on Cemetery ridge at Gettysburg and stared out in the field that is now famous for Confederate General George Pickett's failed charge. Cole had also felt the power of the parks while standing on the steps of the Lincoln Memorial, while imagining what it must have been like to be Martin Luther King presenting his "I have a dream" speech. The parks had the power to make one feel part of something bigger, something grand with purpose and meaning.

This is why Cole had dedicated the last 20 years of his life to the often reviled, underfunded and, in his opinion, underappreciated agency. With every step up the volcano's steep slope he reminded himself how lucky he was to work in some of America's most iconic places. This thought kept him going not only up the mountain, but through the countless budget and staff meetings he was now required to attend. An idea illuminated Cole, perhaps he could hold staff meetings at Camp Muir he bet the meetings would be more brief and the staff would get in better shape. He made a mental note to bring it up to his secretary when he got back to HQ.

Cole had met a lot of mountain climbers in his lifetime. If pressed, he'd guess that many in the climbing community, if not the vast majority, were adrenaline junkies. It came as a surprise to the general public, but mountain climbers weren't necessarily in the sport for environmental reasons. Protecting pretty places and preserving them for future generations he'd found was a fringe cause of the mountain climbing community. The primary focus of many of these groups was assuring and preserving access to the mountain. The climbing community's goal was to bag as many peaks as possible.

But that wasn't the case for Cole, he'd set out today to enjoy the climb, reaching camp Muir was secondary. So, on the way up the mountain, he'd made it a priority to stop and talk to as many people as possible. The new Superintendent was surprised to see there were a fair amount of people both going up and coming down the mountain. On nearly every meeting, Cole would greet the person with a *hello* or *good morning*. He'd always done this when hiking and been asked about it by one of his colleagues many years ago. "Do you expect a greeting in return?"

He'd answered that he hadn't thought about it, but guessed that he did. He really liked saying hello to everyone he passed because where else in our hectic world can one do this and not be seen as crazy? Yet, he really liked the practice because nearly everyone returned the greeting in kind. There was something about being outdoors, being in a national park that made people more receptive to others. Cole found the farther he got from parking lots and front country accommodations the more receptive the average visitor was to engaging in conversation. He loved the license hiking in national parks gave him to honestly engage with others. Again, he'd been hard pressed to find this type of permission anywhere else in the world.

On his climb, Cole had taken the opportunity to engage with several people coming down off the mountain and others completing hikes along the mountain circling Wonderland trail. He'd been interested in hearing how their hike or climb had gone. Everyone had been eager to regale him with tales of adventure and exploration. For some, this was the trip of a lifetime, a bucket list expedition. For others, it was a day trip, something they had done countless times before. Cole wanted to hear their stories. Understanding why people were attracted to the mountain helped him do his job. Their stories revealed what they valued about the place. The mountain's ability to build and maintain strong relationships between people and the environment was a major theme of these stories. Many came to get away from people as well. They wanted the chance to recharge their batteries, examine priorities and reset their life.

Cole pushed on the last several steps to the base camp. Camp Muir, named after famed naturalist John Muir, was a climbing shelter made up of handful of squat buildings and structures. The main camp building was the climber's bivouac. A single story stone and mortar building that looked as though it was right out of the Sound of Music. Adjacent to the main building were a series of smaller structures including a kitchen facility, outhouse, and Park Service communications satellite dish and tower. The tower had recently been put in to improve search and rescue communications and weather forecasts. It had been a controversial addition to Camp Muir, many in the public howled over the "encroachment" of the modern world at their revered base camp, but the NPS reasoned the construction of the tower markedly improved safety at the cost of minimal intrusion.

Cole walked into the Camp and immediately identified the bunk house. He strode the last several feet to the bunkhouse entrance and opened the door. There, inside, he found evidence of previous and recent occupation. A used Cup o'Noodles container, as well as a plastic spoon lay discarded on the floor. Three of the bunkhouse beds were recently used, with mattresses pulled from the other beds. Cole found a crumpled piece of paper on the bunkhouse table. It was an REI sales receipt listing thousands of dollars' worth of recently purchased climbing equipment. Cole presumed they were amateurs as most experienced climbers wouldn't need to purchase everything from ice axes to climbing boots a day before their ascent. Most serious climbers only really begin to trust and feel comfortable with their equipment after several ascents. Yet, according to the receipt, this group had bought everything in Seattle just 24 hours ago. Cole threw the paper and the rest of the trash into a nearby garbage can.

*Odd*, Cole thought. *I could have sworn Beth said there was no one up here.* A slight tinge of disappointment shot through his brain. Cole was really looking forward to some alone time on the mountain. It now appeared he might be sharing the bunkhouse with several people, and from the looks of the bunkhouse's interior, slobs at that. He made a mental note to radio Beth as soon as he got settled in.

Cole dropped his pack near one of the now de-mattressed bunks. He was glad to set the pack down. He was in pretty good shape, but schlepping a 50 pound pack up nearly 5,000ft was no easy task. Besides he wasn't 20 anymore and his body, while still willing, was starting to afflict him with minor aches and pains after strenuous climbs like today.

He grabbed one of the mattresses and replaced it on his claimed bed. From his pack, Cole retrieved his -40 degree sleeping bag and spread it over his bunk. He next pulled out the Park Service climbing, search and rescue and maintenance equipment, as well as food supplies for the camp commissary he'd been asked to carry up to the camp. He spread the items across his bunk and sorted them into piles. He'd carry each pile and place it in the appropriate building.

He next pulled out his radio and checked the strength of his signal. He did a radio check and got a strong signal indication on his radio LED screen. He'd contact Paradise shortly about the unexpected guests, but that could wait a bit longer.

Lastly, Cole removed his 9mm Sig Sauer pistol from the pack. Being a former law enforcement ranger made it seem odd for him to travel anywhere in a national park without his sidearm. However his being the Superintendent meant he had to project a different image, one that was more politician than policeman. So he now rarely wore his pistol on his belt, but he'd be dammed if he wouldn't carry the thing in his pack when traveling in the backcountry. He didn't expect to use the weapon, but old habits die hard.

Settled into his new surroundings, Cole headed back out the bunkhouse to take a look around his campsite for the next couple days. The view was stunning. To the East, Cole could see nearly across Washington State. To the South, the Matterhorn-like Mount Hood in Oregon could be clearly seen, while to the West, the much smaller Olympic mountain range were close enough he felt he could touch them. A hint of the Pacific could be made out just beyond these jagged peaks. To the north, peaks in the North Cascades national park and parts of British Columbia were in view. To the south and west, Mount Adams and Mount St. Helens were shrouded in light wispy clouds, giving the two volcanos a tiger stripe appearance. Cole slowly spun around several times, drinking in the grandeur and the solitude. He would have enjoyed staying in his quiet contemplation for days, that was the plan at least, but it was not to be.

"Superintendent Cole? You there?" came a voice over the walkie talkie strapped to his belt. A voice he recognized as the park dispatcher.

For a moment, he contemplated switching it off, but only for a moment. He pulled the radio from his belt and pressed the call button. "Cole here. What's up Thomas?"

"Hello boss," came the reply. "Sorry to disturb you, but Deputy Superintendent Anderson wanted me to confirm that you had reached camp Muir."

Good old Deputy Superintendent Anderson, always checking up on Cole. Cole couldn't help but feel that Anderson didn't support his being appointed Rainier's Superintendent. Cole had heard through the grapevine at barbeque parties where employees drank and said too much that this might be the case, but Cole had no direct confirmation of his deputy's jealously. So, rather than entertaining the speculation, Cole decided to give his second in command the benefit of the doubt, at least until evidence required him to think otherwise.

"Yep, I made it. Please pass along my thanks to Chuck for checking up on me."

"Will do," Beth answered. "You should also know that we have some weather coming in."

Cole did a quick sweep of the surrounding sky. It was empty except for the veil of clouds around Adams and St. Helens. "Really?" Cole questioned. "Are we sure the report is accurate?"

"Pretty sure," the dispatcher answered. "The National Weather Service is forecasting an 80% chance of thundershowers for tonight. Where you are, that will likely mean snow."

*So, what?* Cole thought. All the better in fact, as it would keep down the crowds. He'd likely have the bunkhouse to himself for the next couple days. "Okay, good to know," Cole replied. "I'll make sure to stay near the bunkhouse this evening."

"Probably smart boss."

Cole was about to ask the young woman if there was anything else when a loud rumble could be heard well up the mountain. It sounded like a thunderclap or perhaps an artillery shell had exploded up slope of his position. Cole turned to see a puff of snow cascading down the side of the peak.

Avalanche. It was thousands of feet away from Cole's current position and presented no current danger. The mass of snow and ice raced down the mountain, kicking up a huge billowing cloud of debris in its wake. From his safe position at Camp Muir Cole was amazed at the apparent slow motion tumble of the snow slide. Yet, he knew that this was an illusion. Avalanches were surprisingly fast and could easily over take even someone on a snowmobile.

As he watched the cascading drama, the new superintendent was quickly reminded of how unpredictable this mountain truly was. Whether it was fast changing weather or unexpected avalanches, this mountain had numerous ways to kill a person.

Cole's radio cracked to life again with the dispatcher's voice. This time it was a bit frantic. "Boss? You seeing that avalanche above your position?"

"Yes, I see it. It's well away from my current location."

"Okay, be careful up there. Along with the new weather information, the park's climbing rangers have revised their avalanche forecasts for the weekend. With the approaching storm they anticipate new snowfall in your location. This will likely increase the avalanche risk," the young woman finished. Before Cole could reply she went on somewhat sheepishly, "Boss? You may want to reconsider your stay."

"Copy." Cole answered, half lost in thought. This trip was getting less relaxing by the moment. Perhaps Beth was right, he'd better bag his weekend getaway and head for lower elevations, no sense taking unnecessary risks. As locals were fond of saying, the mountain would be there in the future, however pushing ones luck may cancel that future date.

Cole was about to radio he was coming down, when he remembered the disheveled bunks and trash strewn around the bunkhouse. Cole glanced off to the West. The wisps of clouds that had just a minute ago been thin smears across Adams and St. Helens were slowly, but surely building, signaling the likely vanguard of the approaching storm front he'd been warned about.

The Superintendent knew changing weather, inexperienced climbers, and the NPS ignorance of their being on the mountain was a recipe for disaster. He'd written the narrative of many an incident report that started exactly that way.

"Beth, thanks for your concern but I've decided to stay. It appears we've got climbers up here that may be in over their heads. I'm going to stick around just in case."

**Paradise Visitor Center, May 4th, Noon**

A non-descript brown domestic sedan pulled into the Paradise visitor center parking lot. Inside, two thirty something white males looked around for a parking space.

The sedan's satellite radio was tuned to a national news channel whose anchor was chattering on about the latest chill over foreign affairs. "In breaking news, tension over the recent breakdown of US/Russian nuclear treaty talks escalated today when the Kremlin announced it was putting its military on full alert and moving some of its mechanized forces forward toward the Polish border."

The sedan's passenger turned up the volume and gave a knowing glance toward the driver, who acknowledged his passenger with a grunt and a nod of his head.

The anchor went on. "In response, US president Paine ordered American forces in both Europe and Asia to full alert. He has also ordered the deployment of two squadrons of the advanced F-22 fighters to Wiesbaden Germany. The president is also deploying America's most advanced stealth bombers to Japan and South Korea in order to counter the building Russian threat."

The two men listened intently as they circled the lot. It was, not surprisingly, packed at this time of day. There didn't appear to be a single available spot anywhere.

Anytime the sun came out in the Pacific Northwest, revealing the majesty that was Mount Rainier, the Paradise visitor center parking lot filled quickly. Even though the lot had recently been expanded to more than 200 spots, much to the dismay of the local environmental groups, the lot still wasn't big enough to accommodate everyone's desire to hike, climb, and play on the sides of an active volcano.

The two men sat in silence as they circled again hoping against hope for an open space. The vehicle's driver noted a park ranger at the far end of the lot directing traffic and obviously alerting drivers to the unavailability of available spots.

His partner saw the ranger as well. A slight hint of concern flashed across the corners of his eyes but, as quickly as it appeared, it vanished. He stuck his hand in his coat pocket to reassure himself that what he put there a few hours before remained in place. It was there.

The radio anchor went on. "The United Nation's general counsel called for both countries to stand down their armed forces and, for the sake of humanity, pull the world back from Armageddon.

Military experts are divided on what will happen next. Theresa Wilmington takes the story from here."

The driver could see the ranger had spotted their circling vehicle. It appeared the ranger was beginning to head their way, obviously intent on shooing them out of the packed lot. He turned the vehicle toward the Paradise Climbing Ranger station. There in front was an open space. The vehicle driver had wanted a less conspicuous space, but beggars couldn't be choosers.

The sound of jet fighters screeched through the sedan's speakers, followed by a female voice the passenger thought had to belong to someone in her twenties. "Standing here on the tarmac of Wiesbaden military airport, jet fighters taking off every 30 seconds one could not be faulted for thinking the world had been transported to the mid 1980's when cold war tension between America and the former Soviet Union were at their highest. According to experts both here in Germany and in the Pentagon, the next 48 hours will be crucial. One critical mistake at this juncture could lead to disaster. However, according to Dr. Samuel Abernathy of George Washington University's school of Domestic and Foreign Affairs, today's foreign policy crisis shouldn't come as a surprise. The United States and Russia have been playing a counting game of chicken for the past several months. Dr. Abernathy predicated back before the turn of the New Year, that the current state of talks would break down. Unfortunately, he was proven correct. The question on everyone's mind now is what next?"

The driver flicked off the radio and pulled into the space clearly marked "For official Use Only!" in large letters.

The ranger saw the vehicle take a government only spot, quickened his pace, and headed in their way.

The two men exited the vehicle, the passenger headed immediately toward the ranger placing himself between the officer and his vehicle.

Both men were exceedingly tall, well over 6 feet in height. They shared a similar slight, lanky build, with arms that seemed a bit longer than normal. Their complexions were pale, bordering on what a layman would consider an albino, yet with a slightly grey tint. The skin resembled the color of off-white or dirty chalk. Both men were clad in completely white high-end climbing attire. The only items that wasn't white were their grey wraparound sunglasses, which protected their vision from the sun's glare but also prevented anyone from getting a good look into their eyes.

"Hello," the passenger said to the approaching ranger. "Good afternoon." He extended his hand offering the approaching ranger a handshake.

"Good afternoon to you," the ranger replied. "How are you gentlemen doing today?" The two shook hands.

"Well. Can't wait to get up on the mountain though," the passenger stated.

"Well that's good. Hey I just want to you to know this parking space is for official use. Only government vehicles are allowed to park there." The ranger explained.

"Totally understand and appreciate the information. However, we are on official government business. See." The passenger stepped aside and pointed to his vehicle.

There on the side of the car was the logo of United States Geologic Service (USGS), the government agency responsible for monitoring the volcanic happenings of the 14,000 foot mountain.

A puzzled look occupied the ranger's face. He did a double take of the USGS sign. "Oh, okay. Can't imagine how I missed that," he apologized. "Sorry to bother you."

"No problem," the passenger answered.

"Have a great morning," the ranger said with a tip of his hat. He took one last puzzled look at the vehicle, turned and headed back to his traffic duties.

The passenger watched him go. *No you aren't wrong my friend,* he thought. *Those markings weren't on the vehicle just a minute ago.* Once the passenger was certain the ranger had returned to his normal task, he turned back to his partner and with an unspoken nod of his head, he acknowledged the driver's quick work on placing the magnetic USGS signs on the side of the car. That should hold off any inquiring minds for the time being. At least as long as the two needed to get up and down the mountain and complete their mission. By the time anyone figured out that the two mysterious visitors really weren't from the USGS, they'd be long gone.

## Disappointment Cleaver Mount Rainier Elevation 12,000 feet, May 4th Noon

Crocker and her team had pushed up the mountain hard for the past two hours. A few more steps and they would clear the final ridge Crocker hoped and believed they'd come face to face with the object she'd been searching for for years. If her hunch was correct, it represented vindication for her dead father and perhaps shake the United States, no the world, to its foundation.

She continued her rest-step climb to the objective. Kick, step, rest. Kick, step, rest. It was the climber's mantra for ascending steep slopes. The rest step preserved energy, which was easily drained on Mount Rainier, while maintaining a steady upward pace. It allows the climber to reach the summit in the quickest amount of time, while expending the least amount of energy.

Crocker realized that the rest-step process was a metaphor for her quest. It had been a long literal and figurative, but steady climb. She was about to reach her objective because of her determination, discipline, and stamina. Crocker found the quest both physically and emotionally challenging. There were countless times when she wanted to quit, to give up the effort, but after a short rest, a resetting of her priorities and a recharging of her batteries, she always came back to the search with even more energy than before.

The recognition that Crocker was on the discovery of something that would change her live and everyone else's on planet earth filled her with energy, pushing her the last several feet to her destination.

She came up over the final rise and gasped. There before her was a fifteen to twenty foot tall black metallic object. As Crocker had guessed when she first spotted it, the object resembled a witch's hat partially buried in the Mountain's glacier ice. Or on closer inspection perhaps it resembled a half buried Egyptian pyramid. The object shimmered in the midday light, yet Crocker could see that it didn't truly reflect the sun's rays. Rather the object appeared to twinkle or radiate like something similar to a heat mirage one might encounter in the desert. As she got closer to the object, Crocker found it hard to actually focus her vision on it. *It must be an optical illusion, yes that's what it had to be* or perhaps the elevation was affecting her worse than she thought. Either way a feeling of unease and dizziness swept over her. She even thought she might retch. She swallowed hard and pushed back the urge. For good measure, Crocker shook her head to clear her senses.

Crocker dropped her pack and was about to approach the object as the rest of her team cleared the last rise.

They too gasped and stood slacked jawed as they took in their first real sight of the object.

"I didn't think it was really up here!" one said.

"Me either," the other agreed.

Crocker's two climbing partners dropped their packs and other equipment next to hers. Crocker dug into her pack to retrieve her digital camera. The light was intense at this altitude and she adjusted her camera lens to accommodate for the glare. However, looking through the camera's viewfinder she found the optical illusion she witnessed with her naked eye was even more powerful. She couldn't get the object in focus using the automatic setting, rather the lenses' servos continually whirred moving back and forth as it tried valiantly but ultimately futilely to bring the object into sharp relief. Again, dizziness swept over her. She closed her eyes tight, and shook her head again. *Ain't that the damndest thing?* Crocker switched her camera to manual and adjusted the lens herself. Yet, despite all her efforts she couldn't bring clarity to the object either. In frustration and despite the rough focus, she snapped a few pictures. She reviewed them in the camera's display screen.

"Crap!" she let out. The pictures on the screen were worse than she would have guessed. The camera clearly failed to capture the object.Rrather a shimmer or ghost of what she knew to be there was all that could be seen. It had a muddied, no fuzzy edge, as if someone had rubbed their finger over the image. The pictures were worthless. She adjusted the lens again, shot several in both manual and autofocus. She changed her position, altering the angle and direction of the sun's light on the object. It made no difference. All the images showed the same thing, a nearly translucent object that apparently didn't want to be photographed, almost like it wasn't there.

But it clearly was there. As hard as it was to look at the object it could be seen and she quickly realized the best way to see it wasn't to directly look at it, but rather to observe it out of the corner of one's eye. This made closely examining the object extremely difficult.

Crocker finally concluded there must be something wrong with the camera. The phenomena affecting her vision must also be altering the camera. She shoved it back in her pack with disgust.

Crocker nodded to her two partners, indicating she was ready to take a closer look. *If I can't photograph it*, she thought, *perhaps I'll return with a piece of it.*

Crocker grabbed her ice axe and began the walk to the object. A distance that couldn't be more than a dozen yards. She was nearly on it when a strange, low level buzz began to be heard. She stopped in her tracks. At first Crocker thought a bee might be buzzing around her. She turned her head and waved her arms to shoo away the wayward insect, but there was no bee. Looking back to her climbing partners, Crocker realized they too heard the buzz. *Weird.*

Convinced there was no insect she moved once more toward the object. The buzz grew louder. In fact, with every step the noise which seemed to be coming from within her head grew louder and louder. She spun around again to face her colleagues. "You hear that?" she asked.

They both nodded yes. Both had a look of confusion and fear on their faces.

*What the hell is going on?* Crocker thought.

**Mount Rainier National Park, 8,000 feet, May 4th, Midafternoon**

After securing their vehicle and throwing on heavy backpacks, the two fictitious USGS agents made quick haste up Mount Rainier's approach to Camp Muir. They set a record pace up the mountain, climbing 3,000feet in roughly 2 hours. They climbed up the slope with the deftness and grace of mountain goats, with nary a misplaced foot or ice ax placement. It was as if the men had climbed the mountain countless times before, despite the fact it was their first ascent. To John Q Public the two men looked like any other park visitor or climber, although they might be a bit more fit than the average hiker. However, to the trained eye the climbers would appear slightly odd. Aside from their breakneck speed and perfect technique, their ascent was nearly a straight line. The men made no accommodation for the terrain or obstacles, they simply went right over any and all things in their path. It was as if they had a set destination and needed to be there at an exact time.

The men made no attempt at switching back or seeking an easier assent. Straight up the mountain they went with speed and determination.

The passenger and the driver had been pushing hard the past two hours. They needed to get up to their objective and back down to their vehicle in 24 hours or less. Time was of the essence and not their friend. Every minute they were on the mountain, in the open really, meant potential discovery, potential disclosure of their actual mission. They couldn't allow this to happen, they couldn't be discovered, no one could know they were on the mountain today.

The passenger, or more precisely the leader of this expedition, stopped for a moment to catch his breath. He and his partner were in extremely good shape, but despite this they hadn't the necessary time to train for what they expected to be a high elevation "recovery". So despite their outstanding physical condition, the mountain's high elevation produced real impacts on their bodies. Olympic athletes even had to prepare for physical exertion at extreme elevation. Unless one lived and worked at altitude all the time, anyone could succumb to elevation symptoms. The passenger knew this and brought plenty of water. Staying hydrated was one way to beat the headaches, difficulty breathing and dizziness that often came with mountain climbing. He and his partner would religiously consume water over the upcoming day. There was too much on the line for them to fail because of a headache.

The passenger removed the cap from his water bottle and downed nearly half its contents in a couple gulps. His partner did the same. He replaced the cap and placed the water bottle back on his belt. He removed a pair of forward looking radar enhanced binoculars. These binoculars were an advanced piece of technology, one that a typical USGS bureaucrat wouldn't have access to. The binoculars didn't provide a visual spectrum image, one that most people are used to from their typical REI field glasses. Rather, these binoculars were designed to pick out heat signatures from nearly five miles away. The passenger credited his foresight for throwing the pair in his backpack, as differences in temperature would easily stand out on a mountain of snow and ice. It would be far easier to find his prey.

He brought the binoculars to his eyes and scanned the horizon looking for any telltale heat index. For several minutes he looked up and down the mountain, nothing appeared out of place. Nothing. He was just about to give up, but chose to train his focus just above Disappointment Cleaver. There, like three stars shining in a pitch black night, the passenger could easily make out three distinct heat signatures. The readout on the binoculars display read these objects were almost 100 degrees Fahrenheit. He used the binoculars 1000x zoom to get a closer look. The image tightened and sharpened, coming clearly into focus. A five year old would easily recognize the three human shapes. He'd hoped this wouldn't be the case. He hoped against hope that his prey wouldn't have made it this far, that they would have given up and turned back, but he knew Aimee Crocker. She wasn't one to quit.

It was just as the passenger had expected, but it was what was just above them on the slope that troubled him the most. There with the three human heat signatures was a fourth object. It was much taller than the humans, roughly the shape of a giant tee-pee. The passenger assumed that it would be nearly impossible to see visually. The U.S. military had been experimenting with light bending stealth technology for years. The ability to hide something in plain sight was getting easier all the time, yet hiding its heat signature had been far more difficult to conceal. All objects must either absorb or emit heat. It's just a fact of life and masking this fact is the holy grail of stealth technology.

The technology hiding the object was good, better than anything he'd seen in his 20 year career. Visually it was nearly undetectable to the naked eye. Like a chameleon, the object seamlessly blended into the mountain's rock and ice, and would have easily remained hidden from the stream of climbers that trekked up and down the mountain over the past seven decades.

But it wasn't perfect. Small ripples of heat could be seen coming off the object. Most wouldn't even notice the effect, but to a trained eye it stood out, like a, "Here I am' sign.

The passenger put the binoculars back in his pack. He signaled to his partner that they were to find cover.

"Let's get going," the passenger said. "Crocker and her team have found the object."

The two dropped their packs and donned snow camouflage suits. They needed to surprise Crocker and her team if they were to be successful. The passenger and his partner had strict "no loose ends" orders. That he hadn't been told what loose ends meant didn't matter. He knew what he must do.

Moreover, the recent breakdown of the U.S./Russian arms control talk had made their mission even more critical and the pressure was mounting to get it wrapped up quickly and quietly. A lot of people were counting on its success and perhaps millions of lives could hang on the balance.

The passenger pondered the ramifications of his task, what would likely happen over the next 24 hours. He knew it was highly likely that people were going to die. That he and his partner were likely going to have to kill several people to protect the secret that until recently was safely buried on Mount Rainier's slopes. The passenger didn't relish this fact, but what was the value of a few lives when compared to millions or perhaps billions?

The passenger pulled a locked briefcase out of his pack. It was roughly half the length of a pool stick and about the size of a coffee table book in width. His partner retrieved a similar one from his pack.

The two opened their cases to reveal SR25 sniper rifles. The rifles were broken down into component parts, which the passenger and driver assembled with military precision and speed. The rifles were all white, painted in typical military arctic camouflage. These men came ready for a winter hunt.

Both slapped a 20 round ammo magazine into the rifle stocks, pulled back the weapons action lever and chambered a 7.62x51 mm round. They retrieved their packs, slung them over their shoulders and stepped out onto one of Mount Rainier's thousands of snowfields.

Now the hard part would begin.

## Disappointment Cleaver, 12,000 feet May 4th, 2:30p.m.

Crocker and her two climbing partners spent the better part of a half hour circling the object. They had walked around its base so many times that they had trampled a well-worn path of its exterior in search of any sign of an opening, any sign of a crack or seem.

Nothing.

It was as if the object was made of a single piece of metal or other material. Rather than being built of metal, it was as if the object had been carved out of a single block. Crocker couldn't quite tell. Crocker wasn't an expert on metals or composite materials but the exterior of the object appeared to be made of a substance not found on earth. It's exterior was a flawless deep black, without so much as a scratch or ding. It cast no reflection and like earlier, when she stared at the object her eyes had difficultly focusing. It was as if she were staring into a pool of perfectly still oil or the vacuum of empty space.

If she hadn't found it herself, Crocker wouldn't have believed that this object had been buried on an active volcano for the better part of six decades. It looked as if it had been placed there just hours before. *Remarkable* she thought.

She touched its smooth exterior; it felt neither warm nor cold. Rather its temperature was consistent regardless of whether she felt a side exposed to the sun or cast entirely in shade. That shouldn't be she surmised. Any object exposed to sun light ought to absorb solar radiation, resulting in a rise in temperature, at least on the side directly in the sun, but that wasn't the case. Crocker stared up at the sun. There wasn't a single cloud between her and earth's nearest star. The sun was beating down directly upon her and the object, but while she could feel the sun's warmth upon her skin, its rays had no effect on the object.

Crocker did notice a slight electric jolt when touching the object, a slight tingle in her fingertips, not quite a shock, rather something more like a tickle. She imagined it was as if while touching the object, it was in turn touching her, almost as if it was aware of her proximity.

Touching the object also produced a distinct taste of metal and the objects buzzing hadn't ended, although the team did notice that it became less intense when one was in direct contact.

*Could the buzzing be some type of homing beacon or perhaps an alarm like warning device?,* she thought.

After several more minutes of fruitless exploration for an entrance or opening, Crocker turned to her team.

"Get the shovels out of the packs," she ordered. "I want to excavate the object's perimeter. Perhaps its hatch or doorway is buried under the ice and snow."

Crocker's teammates did as told and retrieved the tools. She provided them a bit of instruction on what she wanted and at that she and her two teammates began digging a trench around the object. The snow and ice encasing the object were difficult to remove. The fact that the team was working at more than 2 miles above sea-level didn't help either. They were in good physical shape, but this work, an effort to expose a metal object buried high on a mountain under tons of snow and ice would tax even the most fit person. Press on, they did.

While digging, it occurred to Crocker that perhaps this object didn't have a hatch or opening. Perhaps it was something like a drone, a remotely controlled vehicle that required no onboard operator. *But even a drone had to have access panels for maintenance or openings, right?*

The team continued digging for the better part of 90 minutes. Crocker climbed down into the ring of cleared snow that now circled the object. The trench was well over her head. She started walking around the object, inspecting every inch of its exposed surface. Again, her efforts revealed nothing, not a scratch, indentation, or even a mark. It looked brand new.

Crocker made a complete circle of the object, but still found no hatch, no entry point.

"Pull me out," she said to her obviously tired and equally frustrated colleagues.

Her teammates reached down to pull her out, but before Crocker could take their hands, a burst of red exploded from each of their chests. The two fell into the hole, nearly landing on top of her.

Both were dead, their chests opened with single bullet wounds.

## Camp Muir, May 4th, Mid Afternoon

Grayson Cole glanced off to the west. He could clearly see the building storm he'd been warned about earlier in the day. It was a big. Perhaps not by winter standards, but big by late spring standards. It appeared to be shaping up to be a precedent setting event.

Storms were becoming more common in the Pacific Northwest, nearly every season was seeing an increase in the number of squalls. Yet, it wasn't the number that was most troubling, rather it was the intensity of these storms. They carried more precipitation, more energy than similar storms just a few years ago. The larger storms created greater havoc on park resources and taxed the Park Service's ability to respond. Road and trails washed out, bridges were damaged, campgrounds flooded and visitors were often left stranded.

"Damn it," Cole let out. He'd likely have to cut his weekend trip short. He considered waiting out the storm, holing up in the climbers' bunkhouse, but quickly dismissed the idea. If this storm was as bad as it appeared, he could be trapped up at Camp Muir for days. The park would likely be going through emergency procedures without him. He'd be hard pressed to explain to his superiors that he'd decided to stay put and become stranded during a crisis. No, the prudent thing to do, the right thing, was to head down the mountain.

Cole kicked the ground in disgust of his bad luck. The kick sent a cascade of wet snow into the air. Cole stopped. He was obviously worked up and frustrated by the turn in the weather.

When he was a kid, Cole used to work out some of his frustration by playing catch with his friends in the neighborhood. He'd spend hours tossing the ball back and forth until he eventually forgot why he was angry in the first place. Those hours of catch led to a love of baseball and eventually his becoming a starting pitcher on his high school baseball team.

Cole kicked the ground again. Wet clumpy snow shot out from the divot left by his boot. It appeared to be perfect snowball making material. Cole bent down and confirmed his hunch. The snow was perfect. He packed a baseball sized snowball between his two hands, while looking for a target. Could he still throw like he did in high school? He wondered. Did he still have the ability to control his pitches like he did when he was 18?

*Only one way to find out*, he told himself. Cole scanned his surroundings. Roughly 100 feet away he identified a man sized rock sticking straight up out of a snowbank. *Perfect*!

Cole held the snowball in his right hand, while sizing up his rock target. He stared intensely at the rock, going through his throwing motion and seeing the snowball strike the rock in his mind's eye. It was a visualization technique he'd learned from a high school coach, a technique that helped make him a throw better as a pitcher and shoot better as a police officer.

Cole took a deep breath, and went through his wind up, releasing the snowball with as much force and speed as he could muster.

Smack!

The snowball hit the rock dead center. "Woo Hoo!" Cole yelled out a little louder than he intended. He quickly looked around to see if anyone might have heard his unplanned exuberance. He saw no one. "Whew." He let out in relief. "Still got it."

Pleased with his ability to still hit his target, Cole returned to the task at hand and his plans to head down the mountain. He headed for the bunkhouse to retrieve his camping equipment and pack.

From high up on the mountain came a faint crack. No actually two. Cole guessed it to be rock fall. He scanned the mountain but saw nothing, there was no rock fall.

*Odd. If I didn't know better, that sounded like gunfire.*

## Disappointment Cleaver, May 4th, Mid Afternoon

Crocker suppressed a scream. Her colleagues lay dead at her feet. Steam rising from their motionless bodies as the last bit of heat left their remains. She checked the bodies for a pulse, just to confirm her fear. She found nothing.

Crocker's mind raced, what should she do? Someone was obviously out to stop her from learning the truth about the object. She must be getting close to the truth, if they are willing to kill for it.

Crocker knew she didn't have much time. Whoever shot her partners would likely be coming to check their work, and finish off any survivors.

"Think," she said.

Crocker quickly rummaged through her now dead partners' pockets. She found a power bar, a mirror, compass, small Swiss army knife, and a half full canteen. She cursed her luck for leaving her pack on the surface. It held her avalanche shovel, climbing rope, satellite phone, and other survival equipment. She dared not go to retrieve it, knowing the killer or killers were likely bearing down on her position. She'd have to move quickly.

"Where is it?" she cursed. Her breath was becoming labored, she risked hyperventilating. *Calm down!*

She thought. She couldn't afford to panic, not if she was going to stay alive.

She searched her partners' pockets one more time. There on the inside pocket of one of the parkas she found what she was looking for.

A cell phone.

She checked the battery level. Nothing. The phone was dead. Thankfully, she had the spare battery. She'd have to get some distance between herself and the object before she could change the dead battery for the fresh one. But a slight sense of relief came over her. If she could call for help, she might be able to lose her pursuers long enough for help to arrive.

She jammed the phone in her pocket, as well as, the other items she'd pilfered from her companions. Under one of the bodies she spied an ice axe. She grabbed the tool. In a pinch it would make a serious weapon. Better than having nothing more than a boy scout knife to defend oneself.

Over her labored breath, Crocker heard the faint sound of crunching snow. Footsteps! Someone, no two someones were coming.

She frantically looked around. She was still at the bottom of the trench; she had dug over the last several hours. It was unlikely the killers could see her. She was hidden, at least for now. But as soon as they got to the trench and peered down into it, she was as good as dead.

*Think, think, think!* She commanded herself. But there was no more time. The footsteps grew louder. They were almost on top of her.

Crocker snatched up the ice axe and made a decision, she retreated through the trench to the far side of the object. With luck she might be able to crawl out, keeping the object between her and her pursuers, blocking their view of her escape. The killers would want to confirm they had at least two kills. That would take time, a few seconds perhaps, but that would be critical time she could use to slip away.

It was a plan that had little chance of success, but she had to try. She quickly and quietly scurried around the object to the point exactly opposite of where her colleagues lay dead. She tried climbing out of the trench, but failed. The hole was deeper on this side of the object than where her partners lay dead. Even with the ice axe, she couldn't pull herself out. She was trapped.

Crocker froze, mind racing again. *What now!* There was no escape. She frantically looked around for an exit. Anything.

The crunching snow got louder. Then it came to an abrupt end. Crocker guessed the killers had reached the edge of the trench. They were likely confirming their handy-work and quickly realizing the third member of the expedition had escaped. They'd soon figure out where she'd gone.

Crocker began to try an escape with the ice axe again, frantically pounding the snow wall in front of her. Her swings of the axe came to an abrupt end, when she heard her potential killers call out.

"Crocker!" a deep male voice yelled. "We know you are up here! Why don't you come out and save us all some time! You always knew it would end this way, why delay the inevitable?"

## Camp Muir, May 4th, Mid-Afternoon

Cole stopped in his tracks and cocked his head to the left. The noise he'd heard definitely sounded like gunfire. He strained to see if he'd hear the noise again.

Nothing.

He cast his gaze up to where he thought he'd heard the shots. Disappointment Cleaver could clearly be seen in the distance. Cole swore he heard two distinct gunshots, although they had been nearly on top of each other.

Cole pondered his options. He looked off to the west again, the building storm was fast approaching and it looked to be a big one. He then looked back up at Disappointment Cleaver. Someone may need his help, but the noise he heard could just as easily have been rock fall. Many reported that Mount Rainier's falling rocks resembled gun fire.

He strained again to hear anything. There was nothing but the wind which was beginning to pick up. The first indication of the approaching storm.

Cole grabbed his radio and called down to the Paradise ranger station. Perhaps they'd gotten a report of gunfire. Maybe one of his rangers was up on the mountain without his knowledge. Not likely, but it's possible.

"Beth?" Cole started. "Grayson here."

"Yes?" Beth answered. "What's up?"

"Question, are there any rangers up on Disappointment Cleaver today?"

The line went dead. Cole imagined Beth was checking the ranger schedules for an answer to his question.

"Nope, no one is schedule to be up at Disappointment today. Why?"

Cole didn't answer, but instead asked another question. "Have you gotten any reports of gunfire in the park?"

"Gunfire? Beth asked in surprise. "No, absolutely no reports of gunfire. Is everything okay?"

Cole looked up at Disappointment Cleaver again before answering, "I don't know."

## Disappointment Cleaver, May 4th, Mid-Afternoon

Crocker hacked the ice as furiously as she could in a desperate attempt to pull herself from the trench. She'd lost any hesitation to conceal the sound her striking axe was making. She knew it was only a matter of time until her pursuers circled the object and found her. She had to get out. Now.

One particularly violent swing of the ax bounced off the ice and struck the object with a loud clang. Sparks flew from her axe and half its blade broke off and flew through the air. Crocker turned to pick up the broken piece, as a section of the object began to glow.

A low level hiss could be heard coming from inside the object. Then a slight "pop." A distinct section of the object, one that had not been visual just seconds before, opened. A now obvious door moved outward on invisible hinges, stopped and then moved to the right revealing a dark inner chamber. Crocker stared into the abyss with disbelief. She had found an entrance.

"Don't move!" the male voice yelled.

Crocker was shocked out of her attraction to the chamber. For a brief moment, she'd forgotten about her pursuers as she stared into the chamber.

Crocker stared up at two men. They were dressed entirely in white camouflage, something she guessed that was military or intelligence issued. It was obviously high tech, creating an almost translucent effect and making it very difficult to focus on her hunters. Crocker realized the camouflage visual effect was similar to that of the object. Perhaps they shared a similar technology, she thought. Sadly, she'd likely never find out, as it was likely she only had a few more moments to live. If she wanted to extend her life, she'd have to think of something.

Crocker stared at the men, pondering her next move. She noticed nametags with English letters but both the men's names lacked any vowels. It was little more than a jumble of incoherent letters. The insignia's on their shoulders were just as puzzling: a black patch circled in red with the apparently Latin phrase "Si Ego Certiorme Faciam… Mihi Tu Delenous Eris." Crocker had taken Latin in high school and the phrase roughly translated, "We could tell you, but we'd have to kill you." *Great*.

The men's skin tone was equally troubling. It was pale, almost abnormally so. Crocker thought their skin resembled something like milk. She wasn't an M.D. but even to her untrained medical eye the skin appeared to be, abnormally, without pigment. Both men wore wraparound sunglasses, but even despite this she could make out that both men had deep penetrating blue eyes. A blue so deep that Crocker couldn't really make out a pupil. She assumed it was there but couldn't really see it.

Crocker also felt there was something odd about the men's faces. She studied them closely, then it hit her, neither of the men had any facial hair. None what so ever, no beard or mustache, no eyebrows no eye lashes. Crocker assumed they lacked hair on top of their heads as well. It was almost as if the two men had all their hair burned off in a fire that vaporized every follicle but left their skin untouched. *Weird.*

The men also studied Crocker, through their deep blue, unblinking eyes. The paced above her on the trench's ridge. Their movements were efficient and fluid like dancers. Movements of their arms moved like a drape flowing in a gentle breeze, their legs moved with equal grace.

"Who the hell are you?" Crocker demanded. "Why have you killed my friends?"

"Shut up!" the tallest of the camouflaged men yelled. Crocker decided he must be in charge.

"I will not!" Crocker continued. "Who the hell are you?"

"Get her out of that hole, I want to talk to her," the Tall Man said to his colleague.

The slightly shorter man answered with what sounded like "ya" or was it "da"? Crocker couldn't be sure. The choice of words struck her as odd and the shorter man seemed to speak with a bit of an accent. Russian perhaps, but actually impossible to tell given she only heard him utter a single word.

The shorter man jumped down into the trench, appearing to float slightly as he dropped to the ground. He landed with a slight thump. The man was taller than Crocker had imagined, easily over 6ft tall. He grabbed Crocker by the arm.

"Take your hands off me!" she commanded. But despite the man's thin dancer-like stature, he was incredibly strong. He held Crocker's arm firmly. With his free hand, he grabbed Crocker's other arm and proceeded to lift her up from the hole. Crocker tried to thrash her arms, but she was held too tightly. She began to kick and scream, but despite her best efforts, they had no effect on the man. He pushed her up over his head. The taller man had moved to a position directly above Crocker and her captor. The taller man bent down and grabbed Crocker under both armpits and hoisted her out of the trench and threw her in a heap a few feet away. The shorter man scrambled out of the trench and joined his partner. Both towered over Crocker.

The taller man spoke, "You will tell us what we need to know! It is inevitable."

"I won't tell you shit!" Crocker spit back.

Kneeling down, the taller man positioned his face mere inches from Crocker's. He brushed the hair off her face, Crocker recoiled in horror. "Why make this harder than it needs to be?" the taller man said in a now pleasant, melodic tone. "You see my friend over there?" the Tall Man jerked his head toward his partner, "He is very skilled at making people talk."

The shorter man had removed a large knife from the sheath attached to his belt. He wiped it on his sleeve, removing small beads of water from its shimmering blade.

"This can go easy for you, or," the taller man paused for a moment and the went on, "it can go extremely hard. It doesn't matter to me."

He looked around their surroundings. The wind was beginning to pick up and storm clouds could be seen building in the distance. Other than Camp Muir way off in the distance, the area was devoid of human presence and likely would remain that way for the next couple of days. "It doesn't look like anyone will be coming to your rescue, so why don't you do us all a favor and tell us what you know?"

Crocker looked around. The Tall Man was correct, there didn't appear to be anyone within miles of their current position. She might be able to hold out for hours against the expected torture to come, but then what. No one was coming. She was likely dead either way. Her mind raced. *Was there any advantage to withholding what she knew? Was there any advantage to spilling her guts, hopefully not literally? Think, think, think,* Crocker ordered herself.

"Come on! Tell us what we need to know. I promise it will go easier for you."

Crocker swallowed hard. Perhaps she could buy time, at least until the storm blew up. If she could concoct a long, but compelling story, that might just give her enough time.

"Okay," Crocker conceded, "You win. I'll tell you what you want to know."

"Excellent!" the taller man replied with obvious pleasure.

"Where to begin?" Crocker rhetorically asked. "Let's see…"

Just then the wind began to truly pick up. Blowing snow swirled around the three climbers and made it difficult to hear. Snow and ice stung their faces and each instinctively threw their arms up to cover their cheeks and mouths. Crocker paused in her story.

"Come on!" The taller man ordered. "We could freeze out here, waiting for you."

*That's the plan,* Crocker thought. Unfortunately, she'd probably freeze too, but at least she'd have the satisfaction of knowing her captors were also dead.

"Okay," Crocker began again. "Where was I?"

"You have not even started yet." The taller man said annoyance creeping in.

"Right, so it all began back in. . ."

The wind kicked up again. A high pitched howl drowned out Crocker's voice although she continued to talk.

Through the howl a deeper sound could be heard. Crocker stopped talking and cocked an ear to try and identify the sound.

"Go on!" the taller man screamed. He had to raise his voice to be heard over the boiling storm.

But Crocker didn't go on. She knew she had heard something, something like a distant train. Impossible she thought. She was too high up on the mountain to hear a train. Her mind must be going, could the threat of pending death be playing tricks on her? she wondered.

"Enough! You are stalling!" the taller man continued. "You leave me no choice!" He signaled to his partner, who began to approach Crocker. He brought the knife up to her face, mere inches from her eye. Crocker could see in the man's eyes that he was taking pleasure from this. He was going to enjoy torturing her. The determination built on his face, apparently something had switched in his brain. A cold blooded killer now faced her.

Crocker prepared for the first cut. She closed her eyes in a feeble attempt to save her vision. But the cut didn't come. Rather, in the distance she again heard the rumble. It was real and it was getting louder. She opened her eyes and again stared into her attacker's face, but gone was the resolute look of a killer. His look had been replaced by the look, of what she imagined her face to resemble. The look of someone seeing impending death.

Crocker's back was to the building rumble sound. She slowly turned her head. In the distance, she could just make out through the swilling snow, an enormous billowing cloud. It was huge, several stories tall and coming fast. It moved like lightning and roared like thunder. It hadn't been a train she'd heard but this billowing cloud that was racing down upon them.

Her captors stood mesmerized by the fast approaching cloud wall. She imagined they too were stunned and overloaded by what they were witnessing. Crocked quickly looked around. She spotted the trench just feet away. The cloud was almost upon them, the roar now deafening.

*My God,* she thought. It's speed was terrifying. Crocker made a decision. In a flash, she lept into the trench, just ahead of the cloud. She tumbled to the bottom. The cloud raced over the lip of the trench. Crocker was tossed around and battered against the object. She flailed about and grabbed hold of the object's open hatch. The cloud continued to roar over the top of the trench. It was as if someone had opened a jet engine over her head. She could see nothing and hear only it's roar. She imagined the pummeling to what one might experience if trapped within a clothes dryer. She couldn't see anything she couldn't hear anything but the insistent roar. She didn't know which way was up or when the commotion would end.

Snow began to pile up on top of Crocker, threatening to bury her alive at the bottom of the trench. Crocker struggled to hold onto the object while trying to keep from being smothered under the building snow. She felt she was losing the battle. She couldn't hold out much longer. The snow was getting deeper. It was nearly over her head now.

Through the maelstrom, Crocker could make out an object racing down the mountain. It was bouncing right toward her.

A rock!

She struggled to free herself from the trench, but she was buried too deep. She was trapped.

The rock was closer now, barreling down upon her. It was apparent it would strike her. There was nothing she could do to avoid it. She crouched down as best she could, but the snow that was preventing her from escaping was also preventing her from tunneling under as well. It was just too dense. It was only seconds now before the basketball sized rock would strike her. She adjusted her climbing helmet and hoped it would be enough.

The rock continued its race down the mountain, it was moments away now. Crocker closed her eyes and tried like a turtle to pull her head into her body.

Then all was quiet and black.

## Camp Muir. May 4th, Mid-afternoon

Grayson Cole heard the rumble high up on the mountain. It sounded like a train, or multiple cannon blasts. He knew it wasn't a train or even cannons making the noise, rather an avalanche and it was huge and, by the sound of it, probably the biggest he'd ever seen. It was as if the entire upper reaches of the Emmons glacier had broken off and were cascading down the mountain.

Cole grabbed his binoculars and focused on the high up drama. The scale of the event was overwhelming, mesmerizing. Cole thought about how lucky he was to be at Camp Muir which, at least for now, seemed out of danger. The avalanche was up and away from his tiny little base camp.

It immediately struck him that if anyone was up there, they'd be in deep trouble and likely in need of assistance.

Cole continued to watch the sliding snow and ice, it now completely encompassed skyscraper tall Disappointment Cleaver. Like a tidal wave breaking over a south pacific atoll, the cleaver was completely enveloped in snow, ice, and rock. If he didn't know better, Cole wouldn't be surprised to see the Cleaver gone when the avalanche passed.

The avalanche eventually died down, almost as quickly as it had begun. Disappointment Cleaver was still ther, but had obviously taken a beating from the river of snow and ice. Cole continued to scan the aftermath of the avalanche. The upper reaches of Emmons Glacier appeared as if someone had taken a giant backhoe or rototiller and ripped up the slope of the mountain. The jumble of material resembled the remains of a smash up car derby. However, the slabs of ice and rock weren't the size of cars, but instead would dwarf entire buildings or city blocks.

*Impressive,* Cole thought and he once again thanked his stars for not being up on the slope. He was even more grateful that he wouldn't have to travel up there. Cole knew the avalanche slope would continue to be unstable for a while and scanning the upper reaches of the mountain it was obvious the mountain hadn't hurled everything it could down at the cleaver. Much snow and ice remained on the upper reaches of Rainier's slope.

The radio on Cole's belt squawked to life.

"Boss you there?" came Beth's familiar voice through his walkie talkie.

Cole retrieved the radio and keyed the call button, "Yes I'm here."

"Glad to hear it. We've been watching the avalanche from down here as I'm sure you have been."

"Yep, pretty dramatic show," Cole agreed.

"Agree. However, we just got an avalanche beacon warning. It appears someone may be trapped up there."

Cole knew the avalanche beacon was a life saving device many climbers wear. It activates automatically when buried in snow. It allows others to hone in on the signal and recover and rescue survivors. Yet, in order to save avalanche victims, time was of the essence. Many people buried under snow and ice suffocated from carbon dioxide.

He'd have to move quickly.

"Any word from survivors?" Cole asked.

"Nope and we've only received the one avalanche beacon. It's really odd. Almost like the person was climbing alone."

"Possible, but not out of the ordinary." *People do stupid stuff all by themselves in national parks all the time,* Cole thought. "Okay, I'm on my way up. Just need to get my climbing gear, ice axe and helmet. I estimate I'll be up at the site in about an hour."

"10-4, we have also called in an Army National Guard helicopter from nearby Fort Lewis. They expect to arrive about the same time as you. It seems a call to another rescue has slowed down their response. Also, the deteriorating weather may hold them up. There is a real chance they may have to scrub their rescue attempt. If that's the case, you could be up there by yourself for a while."

"Got it," Cole grumbled.

"As a backup, climbing rangers will be heading up shortly. they estimate they won't be on scene for several hours. We will keep you up to date on everyone's progress. You do the same!"

"Okay, Cole out."

Cole replaced the radio on his belt. He headed to the Camp Muir climber's bunkhouse and grabbed his crampons, ice axe, helmet and climbing rope. He also threw several bottles of water into his pack, some food, a camp stove, his sleeping bag, avalanche shovel, headlamp and extra batteries for the lamp and radio, as well as his own avalanche beacon. However, given the situation, it was unlikely anyone would be coming to his rescue for quite some time.

Satisfied he had what he needed Cole left the small bunkhouse and headed up the mountain, up to the site of the recent drama. Exactly to where, just a few moment ago, he'd thanked his stars that he didn't have to travel. He reminded himself not to give thanks early again.

## Disappointment Cleaver, May 4th, Mid-Afternoon

Crocker awoke not knowing where she was. She assumed she was alive, but even that she couldn't be sure of. *Where am I?*

She shook her head, hoping it would clear her mental cobwebs. Big mistake. "Ow!" She yelled.

Her head and neck hurt. She felt as if a truck had hit her. *What happened?* She wondered.

Crocker instinctively tried to reach up and rub her head. But her arm wouldn't move. *Weird.* Yet that was only part of the problem, she realized she couldn't feel her arm at all. Heck, she couldn't feel anything below her neck. She was numb.

Panic gripped Crocker. *I'm paralyzed.* She concluded.

She shook her head again, in an all but vain belief that she could shake herself whole again.

Oddly, it worked. The fog clouding her memory began to lift. She became more aware of her situation.

She wasn't paralyzed at all; rather Crocker was buried nearly up to her neck in snow and ice.

*The avalanche! That's right. I'm buried.*

Her body was still functioning; in fact she was aware of her wiggling toes. She pressed them up against the top of her boots to make sure she hadn't lost her mind. Yes, her toes were working. But she really couldn't feel them. She wasn't paralyzed, she was numb. The snow and ice tomb she was trapped inside had lowered her body temperature and all but disconnected her from anything below her neck.

*This isn't good. I've got to get out of here.*

Crocker tried to free herself from the grip of the snowfield. She struggled to the point of exhaustion. It was no use. She was stuck. It was as if the snow around her had turned into concrete. She couldn't move.

All the thrashing about increased the pounding in her head. It throbbed, each heart beat shooting pain throughout her skull.

Panic again gripped Crocker. She had survived the avalanche, only to awaken stuck high on the mountain to die in a frozen grave.

Crocker was close to the final goal of her quest. If she lived, she knew she could redeem her father's tattered reputation. All she had to do was live.

*Wait*, she thought. *Where is the object?* She'd been hanging onto the object when the avalanche hit, but she wasn't now. She craned her neck to see if she could spot it. She looked to the left, nothing. Then turned her head to the right. Still nothing. She must have been knocked loose from the object. *Where is it? It has to be here.* Crocker thought she hadn't been carried far by the avalanche, but now she wasn't sure. In fact she couldn't be sure how long she'd been unconscious. Had she lost the object of her quest? *This can't be.*

She tried to struggle free again. No use. She was stuck tight. Even worse, she could feel her energy levels dropping. She had no way of knowing how long she'd been out. The sun was starting to set in the West, but was it a different day? She wondered.

She took stock for a moment. She didn't feel hungry or thirsty. That's got to be a good sign she thought. Perhaps I've only been out a short while. But again she couldn't be sure. Perhaps her being numb made it impossible to gauge her appetite.

At that, she started to shiver. The shivering got worse, to the point it was uncontrollable. She knew this was bad. She was becoming hypothermic. She had to get out and warm up quickly, but the harder she struggled, the more stuck she became, and the less energy she had.

It was looking like this was the end. Crocker was extremely tired now, and growing ever more cold. She could no longer feel her legs or arms. It was only a matter of time now. Her vision started to go, but she thought it might be the setting sun and diminishing light.

Her mind started to wander. She was transported back to her childhood. She could see her father at the dinner table pouring over a stack of books and reports. He looked weary, like he had the weight of the world upon his shoulders.

"What's wrong father," Crocker asked.

Her father looked up, but didn't answer. Crocker could see in his eyes that he wanted to tell her something. He wanted her to know something, but what?

Her father pointed to a report on the kitchen table. "What are your trying to tell me father?"

He picked up the report and held it up for Crocker to see. It was a manila folder, like the ones now simulated in Microsoft office. On it was stamped Top Secret, Need to Know Only. The Department of Defense logo was printed on its cover and dated December 1947. She couldn't quite make out the report's title; her father's fingers covered it up.

"Father move your hand, I can't make out the title."

Her father moved his hand revealing the name; Project Blue Beam.

The name didn't ring any bells. "What is project BlueBeam?" she asked. But her father didn't answer. His eyes turned sad and his face and body began to fade.

"Don't leave me father!" Crocker cried out, but he continued to fade. In fact the entire kitchen she had hallucinated began to fade. A darkness was falling over Crocker's vision. Everything was again going to black.

Out of the darkness she could just make out a figure. She squinted to improve her focus. Yes, there was someone out there and they were coming toward her. A halo of light seemed to enshroud him.

In a moment of clarity, Crocker's mind flashed with a realization. *This must be an angel* she thought. *I'm dying. I'm dead.*

The figure continued to approach. Something wasn't right however. It was moving very slowly, almost methodically, in a rhythm. Kick, step, rest. Kick, step, rest. *I thought angels could fly.* Maybe like a Wonderful Life's Clarence, her angel hadn't got its wings yet. *That must be it. Great just my luck to get a wingless angel coming to my salvation.*

*I'm over here* she tried to say, but nothing came out. She had no voice, no breathe with which to make sound, but it didn't matter. The angel seemed to see her. It was waving to her. It got closer and closer. She could now make out its shape a little better. The angel was smaller than she'd imagined, it appeared to be the height of an average man.

*Great, a no-winged, short angel.*

The angel continued its careful approach. It was nearly upon her. The light surrounding it became more intense, but that too was odd. The light wasn't coming from the angel itself but rather from behind it, like a massive light source was behind her savior.

With her last bit of energy, Crocker raised her head to gaze upon her rescuer's face. She couldn't make it out. It was covered in some type of greenish mask. *Odd*, she thought again. The priest and minsters are wrong; angels aren't draped in white, but rather a faded forest green from head to toe. She couldn't make out its eyes; they were hidden behind dark glass. *Perfect. A short, no-winged and poorly dressed angel.*

With her last bit of energy, she lifted her head to gaze upon the angel's halo. She could make it out clearly. A flat, tannish, crown that engulfed and ringed the angel's head. *Well at least it has appropriate head gear.* Her consciousness was drifting away, she was nearly gone. The shivering had stopped. She couldn't feel her body anymore. She was ready to go.

She looked up at the halo one last time and thought it looked like something Smoky Bear might wear.

## Disappointment Cleaver, May 4th, Late Afternoon

Grayson Cole checked his homing equipment one last time. The avalanche beacon was transmitting perfectly the signal coming in loud and clear, and as indicated on the homing device's screen should be just a few dozen yards ahead.

Cole pulled out his binoculars and scanned the nearby snowfield. It was a jumble of snow, ice and rocks, resembling to all the world as if a giant had just worked the area with a massive plow. Rocks dozens of feet tall, intermixed with house size blocks of ice were scattered far up and down the mountainside. Cole thought to himself that it would be a miracle if anyone survived the slide.

He checked the homing device again. The signal was strong and just ahead. He set out toward it. Cole was grateful the sun was directly behind him. This should make it easier for him to spot someone without his having to strain against the blinding sunlight. He hoped perhaps that some reflector or other shiny object might give off a flash for him to hone in on.

But this might not be the case, so he yelled out to anyone who might be able to hear him. His voice felt small and lost on the vastness of Mount Rainier. His yelling out was like throwing a rock in the ocean in the hope of stopping the waves. But he had to try.

The snowfield was larger than he imagined. And because Cole knew about avalanche survival, he knew time was running out. The victim or victims could be suffocating from a lack of oxygen, have internal or external injuries, be suffering from hypothermia or all of the above. He needed to find them quickly if there was any hope to save them.

Cole reached the edge of the avalanche field. He looked up the mountain assessing the potential risks of future slides. However, it appeared this avalanche had emptied the field of any snow that could trigger or be used in a pending slide. He took a bit of comfort from this fact. However, he'd still have to find his victim in the proverbial haystack.

He looked over his shoulder and could see the sun was fast setting. He'd likely had only an hour or so of daylight left. He needed to find the climbers soon, triage and treat their injuries before sundown. He'd also have to construct shelter, given the helicopter may not make it before dark. It was a lot to do, and time kept ticking.

Cole stepped into the avalanche field and immediately realized the scope of the task ahead of him. The boulders and ice blocks created a virtual maze and reduced his sightlines to a few feet on several occasions. It was like searching a carnival fun house. He'd almost need dumb luck to find anyone in the mess. He'd have to trust the homing device.

He checked it again. The signal was still coming in loud and clear. The homing device's screen flashed the location of the beacon as tantalizingly close. A mere dozen yards as the crow flies. As Cole raised his head, that dozen yards would likely take him an hour to traverse, with nearly insurmountable boulders and ice blocking his path.

The gauntlet reminded him of the thorny briar bushes which blocked Prince Phillips rescue of Sleeping Beauty. Thankfully, he thought to himself there was no Maleficent conjured dragon also standing in his way.

Cole stepped up to one large ice block and tried to move around it. But regardless of whether he traveled left or right, the path was blocked. He'd have to climb over it. Cole let out a low sigh. *It was never easy, was it?* he thought to himself.

He quickly put the thought out of his head. He had no time to waste. Cole grabbed the ice axes from his belt, he thanked his lucky stars that he'd thought to bring two. He swung the first one and sunk it deep into the ice block's sheer face. The axe went in surprisingly easy. This was good and bad news. The soft ice should make climbing relatively easy. However, that softness would also mean the ice was unstable. It could come crashing down at any moment.

*Again, it couldn't be easy could it?* he asked himself. *I wouldn't have it any other way.*

Cole checked his feet to make sure the crampon spikes strapped to his boots were secure. These spikes would have to hold his weight. His life depended upon these little pieces of steel.

*I hope the person who made my crampons had a good day that day*, Cole thought.

Cole faced the ice wall. He moved his hips away from the ice to look down at his feet. He carefully searched the wall with the finger length toe points on his left boot. Finding an adequate spot, he kicked the points into the ice. They sunk deep providing a secure step. Cole repeated the process with his right foot, searching for a step roughly the same level as left foot. He kicked in and these spikes went in easily as well.

Cole moved his hips closer to the ice and swung the axe in his right hand. It too sunk deep into the wall. Cole repeated the process on moving his feet, swinging the axes for 15 minutes. He'd climbed over half way up and dozens of feet above where he'd started his climb.

The ranger was preparing to move his feet again, when he felt the ice block move ever so slightly. Cole's heart skipped a beat. He could feel a surge of adrenaline shoot through his body. He froze and stopped his climb to further assess the situation.

*Was the ice block moving?* Cole thought. *Or was it the mountain moving?* Earthquakes were common on Mount Rainier. Cole continued to hold his position.

Cole was about to resume his climb when the ice block began to slowly tilt to the right. The ice block was moving.

"Shit!" Cole let out. He squeezed his body as close to the ice as he could. He wished he could transform into a spider or ant and really get a hold of the wall.

The block continued to shift and its speed started to pick up. If it continued to fall, Cole would likely be crushed by the hundred ton block of ice.

There was little the ranger could do. He was little more than a flea on the side of an ice leviathan.

Yet, as quickly as the ice wall began moving, it stopped with a sudden jerk. Cole was nearly thrown from it. His feet lost their hold on the wall and Cole's hold on his ice axes was all that kept him from falling to his death. His legs flailed under him and he swung out and away from the wall. He slammed back against the wall with a thud. Cole knew that would hurt later on.

Ice and rock that had been dislodged by the ice block's violent lurch began to cascade down upon Cole's head. He instinctively tried to pull his head into his body. Large rocks and ice blocks rained down past him. A large block about the size of a small car missed by inches.

Smaller baseball chunks of ice and rock continued to rain down. Several striking his helmet covered head. Cole continued to hold on for dear life.   A large rock hit Cole squarely on the top of his head. His helmet split nearly in two. Once again the ranger lost his footing and clung to the ice wall by his two small axes. His vision filled with stars and he felt as if he were floating.

Cole shook his head to clear out the cobwebs. He regained his senses, but while his senses had returned to him the overall situation hadn't improved much.

Snow, ice, and rock continued to rain down. Cole decided he couldn't stay where he was any longer. It was only a matter of time until he was knocked off his tiny perch.

Cole could see he was only a few yards from the top of the ice block. He pushed and scrambled his way up the last several feet. He reached his hand up to reach over the top of the ice block and pulled himself up on top of the block. He collapsed onto its surface, confident in the fact that he was safe for the moment.

CRACK!

Cole searched the surrounding area for the noise source. He found it quickly.

A third of the ice block, the third he was resting on, was breaking away from the larger block. Cole scrambled to his feet and began to run toward the widening crevasse.

Cole's crampons made it difficult to run. His spikes caught on several steps and sent the ranger tumbling to the ground.

CRACK!

Like a block of wood being split by an invisible axe, the ice block was cleaving into two parts. Cole was about to cascade back down the face of the ice block he'd just climbed.

*Faster*! He thought.

Cole picked up the pace. The crack could be seen just ahead. And like a scene out of a disaster movie, the crack was growing, spreading across the entire roof of the ice chunk. It was a few inches across, now a foot, now two feet.

Cole calculated that by the time he reached the crack it would be yards across. He knew he'd have to jump the chasm. Cole quicken his pace even more. Pumping his arms and lifting his knees. The crack continued to grow. Yet now the piece Cole was running on began to fall. It was only a matter of seconds before it completely dropped away.

Cole raced to the edge of the crack, it was bigger than he'd imagined, but there was no time or place to turn back now. He jumped!

Cole flew through the air. He did his best Jessie Owens long jump, quickly realizing that the Olympian likely didn't make his record jump with 30 pounds of equipment and cold weather gear on. Although, it occurred to Cole that Owens likely could make this jump even if he had been so clothed.

Cole took a quick glance into the fissure he was flying over. It stretched deep into the snowfield. If he didn't make it, no one would ever find his body.

The leap took every bit of the ranger's energy and strength and still wasn't enough. He came up just short, hitting the far side of the divide mid-chest. Cole's legs dangled into the breach, while his arms landed on the top of the ice block.

Cole kicked wildly with his boots in a violent effort to gain a toe hold on the sheer ice wall. His crampons found purchase and prevented the ranger's fall. Cole used his ice axes to slowly crawl his way out of the hole. Eventually, he pulled himself up and onto the top of the block. He caught his breathe and once again took a moment to survey his situation. He let out a deep breathe, looking up to the sky he thought, *It can never be easy.*

The storm to the west was still building and would likely be on him in minutes not hours. He'd have to find the avalanche victims and soon. Otherwise, they'd likely freeze to death in the impending storm. *If they weren't already dead*, he thought to himself.

Cole scanned to the north and east toward the direction of the beacon signal. He used his binoculars to search the nearby debris field. After a few minutes of searching, he spotted something that appeared promising. A climber's helmet. It was nearly submerged in a snowfield. But it was obviously a helmet. The question now was, was it attached to anyone?

Cole retrieved his homing device and focused it on the helmet. The signal came in loud and clear. The helmet and the avalanche beacon shared the same location. That was good news. If his luck held out, he could retrieve the victims and get his shelter built before the pending storm. He'd have to move fast.

He replaced the homing beacon back on his belt and placed the binoculars in his pack. He headed down the far side of the ice block that had nearly been his tomb. It's backside was steeper than anticipated and required Cole to slowly and carefully make his descent. He nearly stumbled on a couple occasions, which caused Cole to think he looked quite the awkward savior to anyone who might be tracking his progress. But avalanche victims can't be choosey about who rescues them, he told himself.

Cole finally reached the bottom of the ice block and stepped onto a flat plain that appeared unaffected by the recent avalanche. On the far side of the snowfield he could still make out the climber's helmet. It was still sticking out of the snow, and appeared to be moving. Cole stared more intently.

Yes, it was moving! It could be the wind he told himself, but nonetheless he picked up his pace.

The snowfield he crossed was roughly a couple dozen yards across. This was more good news. It appeared large enough to land a helicopter, which Cole would need if he was going to get the survivors off this mountain in time to save their lives.

Cole adjusted his helmet which had slid to one side of his head, but it was badly damaged and nearly fell apart. Cole cursed under his breath. But there was no sense in crying over spilt milk. He'd have to make do without the helmet.

He removed it from his head and pulled the headlamp from it. He'd need his flashlight as the sun was setting fast behind the bulk of the mountain. It was going to get dark and cold real quick.

Cole tried to adjust the lamp to his head, but its straps had also been damaged in the rock fall. The lamps straps were too loose to stay on his head. He grabbed his Stetson from the back of his pack, and put the headlamp on his flat hat. It fit, not perfectly, but well enough.

The buried victim was clearly visible now. He could see it was a woman, likely in her late 20s or early 30s. She'd stopped moving. Cole quickened his pace.

## Columbia Ice Field, May 4th, Early Evening.

The Tall Man awoke to find himself buried under a blanket of snow. Thankfully, he'd been able to stay near the avalanche's surface and with a little effort he was able to free himself from a snowbank. He did a quick self-assessment to see if anything was broken or injured. Except for a minor cut on his chin and a few other bumps and bruises, he appeared okay. He did a quick check of his equipment including his binoculars, radio, and sidearm. They too appeared in working order. However, he'd lost his rifle. It had been pulled from him in the jumble and torrent of the avalanche. It could be anywhere on the mountain and he didn't have time to look for it.

The Tall Man realized he hadn't heard from his partner. He scanned the surroundings but found nothing. The avalanche field was huge, stretching miles both up and down the mountain. His partner could be anywhere. It occurred to the Tall Man that it was also likely he was dead. He put the man out of his mind and returned to his task at hand. He grabbed his binoculars and scanned up the mountain focusing on where he believed the object was located.

He found nothing. It was gone. *Could it have been swept away? Or was it buried now under tons of snow and ice?* He also searched for Crocker but couldn't find her either. *Hopefully, she'd been killed in the avalanche.* That would solve many of his problems, but he couldn't assume it was the case. In fact, he'd have to assume she was still alive and likely scrambling to get back to the object.

The Tall Man made a decision. He assumed his partner was dead and even if he wasn't he didn't have time to search for him. Rather, he readjusted his backpack and started out toward the spot where the object was last located. By his reckoning he'd fallen about a 1,000 feet from his previous location. It would take him much of the night to make up that lost ground. He'd have to move fast and now if he was going to stop Crocker and fulfill his mission.

## Disappointment Cleaver, May 4th, Early Evening

Cole found his first victim buried to her neck in snow and ice. She was unconscious and unresponsive. He immediately checked for vital signs, determining her pulse and breathing were weak and labored. She was obviously in distress. Cole assumed her body temperature was also critically low.

Cole began setting up his tent shelter. He'd need to get this woman into a warm environment and raise her body temperature as soon as possible. It took him only a matter of minutes to set up his state of the art tent. It was new technology that no matter the outside temperature stayed toasty on the inside. Cole had no idea how it was done, but didn't care, and believed this technology would save countless critically cold hikers and climbers.

The tent went up in a matter of seconds. Cole had practiced the exercise countless times. He'd been caught in plenty of downpours with the need to set up shelter quickly and easily. He'd learned several tricks along the way that allowed for near Olympic speed. He paid particular attention to wind direction, making sure the tent doors where perpendicular to the building gale.

After driving in the last tent stake and determining the shelter was secure, he grabbed his avalanche shovel and began to dig his victim out of her icy tomb. She

125

had obviously been in the slide for some time, perhaps 30 minutes and was lucky to still be alive. If she hadn't been able to keep her head above the surface, Cole guessed he'd likely now be digging up a corpse, but she'd been skilled or extremely lucky managing to avoid the grim reaper.

He kept digging; eventually freeing the young woman from the snowbank. He did a quick scan of her body to determine if she had any broken bones, bleeding, or bruises. He saw nothing obvious. *Good news*, he thought.

He ran a thermal thermometer across her forehead. What it read shocked him, 92 degrees. Cole knew hypothermia, the deadly extreme cooling of the body started at 95 degrees. If Cole didn't get her core body temperature warmed up immediately, this woman likely had minutes to live.

Cole broke out a couple hand warmers he'd packed for this situation. They were the type of over the counter chemical warmers, popular with hunters and football fans. They'd do the trick of stabilizing the patient. But Cole knew he didn't have enough time for warmers to do their magic. More drastic action would have to be taken.

Down at the Paradise ranger station, if this woman had been brought to the first aid station, the rangers would have raised her body temperature by putting her in a warm bed, in a warm room while trying to get warm liquids into her body. Cole had none of these things.

He'd have to improvise.

Before going forward though, Cole quickly searched the surrounding slide area to see if any other victims were buried nearby. He found no one.

He turned back to his victim. He pulled her into the tent and positioned her on top of the zipped open -20 sleeping bag. He applied heat packs to her shoulders, arm pits, and groin. Cole wrapped her in a space blanket, a kind of aluminum foil designed to prevent heat loss. He placed his heavy coat over the patient, as an extra level of protection.

Before zipping up the sleeping bag, Cole grabbed his thermometer and took one last temperature reading. It still read 92 degrees. Things weren't improving. Cole had recently renewed his Wilderness First Aid training and learned that in severe cases of hypothermia, body to body contact with the victim can be effective.

Cole climbed into the sleeping bag with his patient and zipped it shut. It was a tight fit and after a few minutes in the bag, it started to get stuffy.

Despite his patient being bundled in heavy mountain climbing clothes, and wrapped in a space blanket, Cole could feel she was physically fit. Her legs and arms were well defined and her stomach and chest were firm. She'd obviously trained for this climb. That was a good sign, it would improve her chances of surviving the cold.

Cole felt a bit odd, climbing into a sleeping bag with such an attractive woman, especially given that she was unconscious. He knew he had to do it, but he hoped she would understand his thinking when she regained consciousness.

Outside the tent, the wind began to pick up. As predicted the building storm had finally arrived. The tent's walls began to buffet and whip. It would be a very long night, Cole realized.

He settled into the cramped sleeping bag as best he could. His patient's breathing continued to be labored, but it seemed to be improving. At least he hoped it was.

As the sun finally set, Cole was all but alone in the dark. He could feel the victim's chest rising and falling, but he could no longer hear her breath over the raging storm, at least not unless he pressed his ear up next to her mouth.

In the darkness, the ranger slowly realized how tired he truly was. It had been exhausting both physically and mentally getting to his patient and pulling her from the avalanche. Sleep was going to overtake him shortly.

As he dozed off, Cole convinced himself that his patient's respiration and temperature was improving. At least it better be. The temperature was dropping fast outside his tent. Cole slowly understood it would be a while before help arrived. If he didn't stabilize his patient in the next eight hours, it wouldn't matter when his backup arrived. Even worse, as the temperature dropped outside his tent, Cole finally fell asleep to the apprehension that, even despite his best efforts, the rescue team might find not one, but two corpses in the tent.

**Emmons Glacier, May 4ᵗʰ, Evening**

The Tall Man had been caught out in the open when the predicted storm finally hit. He had only a few minutes to get his tent up before the storm's real power and fury hit. His was a state of the art winter shelter, developed by the Department of Defense's Advanced Research Projects Agency (DARPA). The two person shelter went up in seconds and incorporated technology that heated the tent from solar energy. The shelter's surface was coated with light absorbing material, making it nearly invisible. It was a perfectly camouflaged shelter, using technology that was 20 years ahead of its time.

The military had thousands of these types of gadgets using advanced technology. DARPA was a relatively unknown agency. Its primary mission was to conduct research and develop technology and projects that could expand military capabilities. Light bending, nearly perfect camouflage was just one of the publicly unknown DARPA advancements, but it wasn't the only one; it wasn't even close to the most advanced or cutting edge.

The United States had been caught with its scientific pants down, when the Soviets were the first to successfully launch a satellite into space. DARPA was created so that America would never be taken scientifically or technologically by surprise ever again. And since DARPA's founding in 1958, this had been the case. Since then, DARPA's best known advancements included things such as the internet, stealth technology, and unmanned military drones.

The Tall Man had played a part in each of these projects, and many yet unknown developments. Pending projects that would boggle the mind, shake conventional wisdom, and seem to violate our common sense understanding of the universe. In the right hands, this technology could bring incredible societal benefit. In the wrong hands however, this technology could destroy humanity and much of the rest of the world's lifeforms.

Yet, the Tall Man knew that the world had changed since he first got involved with DARPA. It started at the end of World War II with the development of atomic bombs. Then it changed again with the creation of hydrogen bombs. These bombs made the Hiroshima and Nagasaki explosions seem like children's fireworks. The world changed again with the Russian's detonation of its own nuclear device, followed soon after by the Chinese, British, East Indians, French, Israelis, South Africans, Pakistanis and North Koreans. The atomic genie could never be put back in the bottle. Multiple countries and now even multiple independent agents played in the advanced technology arena. DARPA's job was to stay at least one step ahead of these various other actors.

To date it had succeeded. But it wasn't like the Tall Man could take any solace in this impressive record. He knew all too well that a single mistake, just one failure to stay ahead of the nation's enemies could mean the end of the United States and freedom loving people everywhere.

The unwritten moto of his DARPA team was, "Victory was temporary, defeat was permanent." That was the mantra that pushed his staff to stay ahead of its opponents.

Ever more destructive bombs were just part of the team's research. It divided its time almost equally between offensive and defensive weapons systems. So one day, the Tall Man worked on stealth technology that could defeat the best radar systems, the next on radar systems that could detect the best stealth weapons.

Eventually it dawned on the Tall Man, his team, and the rest of his higher ups in the federal government that they were approaching a point of no return, a critical mass so to speak. He feared his team or another in DARPA would produce a weapon so powerful that no defense system could counter it.

This wasn't really a new fear. The Manhattan Project scientists, the men and women who built the world's firsts atomic weapons, once worried that their weapons had become so powerful that there was the minor chance that detonating one would ignite the earth's atmosphere and kill every living thing on the planet. But despite this fear, they went forward with their test anyway. That the atmosphere didn't ignite only emboldened these men and women. They pushed forward and pushed the scientific envelop creating atom smashers so powerful that some worried that once powered up, the smasher would create a mini black hole and crush the earth. Again, the scientists pushed forward and dodged another bullet of Armageddon. Many believe the mythical doomsday weapon would never be developed. No matter how powerful a bomb, atom smasher or any other weapon, there would always be a counter. For every sword, there was an equal shield.

The Tall Man wasn't convinced. He knew that it wouldn't take a single doomsday weapon to wipe out the planet. Use of conventional nuclear weapons were more than up to the task and given the failure of states like the Soviet Union, the materials needed to construct these horrifying weapons were spreading among a growing number of countries. The United States, as well as, the United Nations did their best to prevent nuclear proliferation, but the genie was nearly impossible to contain, to say nothing of putting it back in the bottle. So millions were spent on missions to track and secure any stolen nuclear material. Special Forces delta squads were on 24 hour notice, ready to reacquire the nuclear material by any means necessary, anywhere, at any time. Unknown to the general public, the Special Forces had been dispatched on more missions than the Tall Man cared to think about. It was only a matter of time until a disaster happened.

There was no weapon or shield that could be deployed to prevent this future the Tall Man concluded. At least not a conventional one. No, the Tall Man was convinced the best way to prevent humanity's destruction was through the combination of technology and psychology. The enemy had to believe their very existence was in doubt. That once the bombs started flying, there would be no winners. No real survivors. If an enemy could be convinced that warfare was futile in the first place, they likely wouldn't start down the path.

History was replete with countries that had placed faith in a similar strategy. The countries of 20th century Europe had believed in what turned out to be a mistaken idea that war had become too horrific and costly that no one would be so foolish as to unleash the deadly technology of machine guns, airplanes, and poisoned gas upon them. Their faith in the rational action of their opponents had been wrong and World War I was the result.

Not wanting to make the same mistake, a mistake in the believing in the better intentions of one enemy, after World War I, countries like France spent millions on defensive bunkers, fixed artillery cannons, and fortified strongholds. The Maginot line as it was called, was France's response to the failed hope of calmer heads prevailing.

But like 30 years before, Europe's belief that war would never come again had been wrong. The Nazi's simply went around the French's Maginot line and defeated its historic enemy in a matter of weeks. At the end of the war, tens of millions had been killed and millions more displaced. It would take Europe and Japan decades to recover from the conflict.

The Tall Man was troubled by a similar line of thinking and faith in the idea that no one would be stupid enough to start a nuclear war growing among world leaders. At countless Washington DC cocktail parties, the Tall Man had lost count of how many congress members, high level administrative officials, media types, and others stated no country would be crazy enough to start a nuclear war.

The Tall Man knew this thinking had permeated other countries as well. Be it diplomatic missions to Moscow, scientific conferences in New Delhi, or cultural exchanges in Beijing the message was always the same. Surely we are smarter than our ancestors;

we would never make the mistakes of our 19th and 20th century counterparts and never engage in all-out war.

These people clearly didn't know their history, and that was bad. For these people were the world's elite, and if they couldn't see the flaw in their logic then planet earth was in grave danger.

Eventually, the Tall Man was convinced the current strategy and thinking would fail. It was like watching a bus full of children driving toward a cliff, while everyone standing around placed faith in the fact that surely the bus would swerve and avoid the calamity, but the Tall Man knew, unless something drastic was done, the bus would drive off the precipice. He knew he had to do something different.

He was reminded of the Einstein quote that the world can't solve its problems by using the same logic and thinking used to create them. New thinking, new approaches, new and bold action would have to be taken.

But what? That had been the key question and the goal of the super-secret Majestic 12 group, formed by an executive order signed by Harry Truman right after the war.

Almost from the beginning of his association with the federal government, the Tall Man had been part of

Majestic 12. He'd been identified as a critical need for the team, an off the books committee of scientists, government officials, and military leaders whose purpose was to protect national security in ways that required new thinking and new approaches. The Tall Man fit right in.

If Majestic 12's mission was to prevent world war III, the Tall Man knew he had "unique" experience and qualities that would make him exceptionally qualified to help Majestic achieve its mission.

In one of his first meetings with the team, the Tall Man was asked if he wanted to put his ideas into practice. Did he want to work with the best scientific minds on new ways to stop war before it started?

Of course, came his response.

That was decades ago.

At first he'd been told he'd assume a fairly regular life. He'd be contacted in good time about where and when he'd be "activated."

He had been required to leave his friends and previous life behind. It wasn't too difficult as he had very few friends and not much of a life to leave behind, but for all intents and purposes he no longer existed. He was no longer subject to national or even international law. He was above it, no beyond it. He moved around the globe without leaving any trace. No digital footprint, no paper trail. Total anonymity.

It was lonely at first, and his first several "missions" seemed pointless. They were little more than information gathering. He'd been on several covert surveillance operations in those early years of what he considered conspiracy nutjobs. He'd been forced to attend conferences with remote viewing experts, anti-vax proponents, and UFOlogist. When not attending the meetings of whackjobs he'd spent hours pursuing government records and national and international media looking for stories and reports on aliens and UFOs.

He'd begun to suspect that he had been the subject of an elaborate ruse, that someone high up in the military was playing an extravagant and expensive trick on him. The Tall Man had decided to walk away from the farce when he was finally let in on the secret, the new thinking that was to prevent and would continue to prevent world war III.

When it was explained to him it seemed ridiculous. The idea was so preposterous that it couldn't succeed. It required subterfuge and misdirection, when being direct was required and likely more effective. The more he sat with the plan, the more he considered its military, political, economic, and even psychological ramifications. He came to the conclusion that it was actually the only way to prevent humanity's annihilation.

He committed himself to the cause ever since, but in one sense, he didn't really have a choice. For all intents and purposes he owed his life to the federal government. That debt would one day be repaid, but that was an issue for another day.

The Tall Man opened his backpack and spread its supplies across his sleeping bag. He'd lost some of his equipment in the avalanche, but he still needed to finish his assignment.

On the sleeping bag, he laid a high tech pair of night vision binoculars. He placed these next to his high powered satellite walkie-talkie/weather radio. He next pulled out his 9mm Glock semi-automatic pistol. He had four additional ammunition magazines, including the ten rounds in the pistol's handle. He had 50 bullets. That should be more than enough to take care of Crocker he thought.

The Tall Man pulled out what little food he had. Some crackers, three cans of smoked salmon, two freeze dried meals, one spaghetti with meatballs, the other beef stew. He also had a couple power bars and a pouch of trail mix. If he rationed it out, there was enough food to last several days. He cursed under his breath for not having more. However, he hadn't expected the mission to take more than a couple of hours. It should have already been over with he and his partner well on their way out of Washington. It hadn't worked out that way.

He next grabbed a flashlight from his backpack, followed by a small camp stove with a day's supply of fuel and a water proof container of matches. He also had two canteens of water, one about a quarter full. Again, he cursed his bad luck. He hadn't counted on being out so long. Besides, if all else failed he could melt snow on his camp stove and drink that. He would only do that as a last resort, as the flame from the camp stove might give away his location.

He next pulled out four half pound plastic wrapped packages. They appeared to be packages of modeling clay or playdoh, but these weren't toys. Rather they were 2 pounds of military grade C4 high explosives. In his pack he had the ability to destroy a small plane or vehicle. He checked his supply of blasting caps and their wireless detonators. All seemed to be in working order.

Finally, he pulled out 6 grenades. He separated them by type; two concussion, two smoke, one flashbang and one electromagnetic pulse. He gently placed them on his sleeping bag. He checked each explosive making sure they were undamaged. He gave particular attention to the EMP grenade. This device, about the size of a Coke can could take out enemy electronics like night vision googles and GPS systems. It would come in handy if he came across a superior force.

All grenades appeared to be in working order, but he had no real way of testing them. He'd have to trust them if and when the time came.

He'd lost his rifle, but still had ammunition for it in his pack. It was basically worthless now, but he'd keep it just in case.

He carefully replaced everything in his pack, all except the satellite walkie-talkie/weather radio. He pulled out its ear piece and carefully inserted it into his ear. He turned on the radio and tuned it to a local news radio station. The announcer was warning everyone about the building storm and that all should seek shelter, stay off the roads, and stay indoors until it passed. It was estimated the storm would last through the next couple of days, with a small chance of localized clearing late tomorrow.

"Hmm," the Tall Man muttered.

If there was a clearing tomorrow, there was an off chance that Crocker could get off the mountain with whatever she may have recovered from the object. He'd have to push on first thing tomorrow, despite the weather. If his partner had survived the avalanche, he would have pushed on tonight, but it was too dangerous to venture through blinding blizzards, on snowfields, and over crevasse riddled glaciers by oneself. One could easily fall into a crack in the ice or step off a thousand foot cliff and never be seen again. The Tall Man couldn't risk that. He had to finish the job.

The announcer finished her weather report and at the top of the hour, an announcer with the national broadcast came on to give the latest news. Not surprising the growing tension between Russia and the United States dominated the report. The Tall Man turned up the volume.

"Talks between Russia and the United States over nuclear arms reduction broke down today," the male announcer began. "Russian negotiators stormed out of the meeting. Immediately thereafter, Russian military forces were placed on high alert. NATO commanders in Germany report Russian armored divisions and infantry units have been moved up to the border of Ukraine and Belarus. American negotiators are not optimistic about their Russian counterparts returning to the table anytime soon. Let's bring in Sarah Mitchell at this point who is standing by at the Pentagon."

"Thanks Tom," from her voice the Tall Man estimated the reporter was probably 20 something. "The Secretary of Defense announced today that in response to our European and Asia allies requests, who are rightly worried about the Russian's moving forces to their frontiers, he has placed American forces in Europe and Asia on a similar war readiness. In particular, armored divisions in Europe have been placed on high alert. In South Korea, American forces are under similar orders. Meanwhile, three aircraft carrier task forces are moving into positions around the former Soviet Union. The USS Nimitz, out of Bremerton Washington, is steaming toward the northern Pacific to patrol an area off the Russian Kamchatka peninsula. The George Bush is positioned in the Mediterranean, while the Theodore Roosevelt is cruising to the Baltic Sea."

"What about Air Force units?" the male anchor asked.

"A squadron of stealth fighters and long range bombers at Germany's Ramstein Air Force base are gearing up, while predator drones are patrolling the air space over Turkey, a NATO ally."

The anchor cut in again, "How have the Russians responded to America's actions?"

"Not surprising, the Russians have responded in a similar fashion placing their naval and air forces on alert. American military experts have told me that the world has not seen a comparable emergency since the Cuban missile crisis."

The Tall Man shut off the radio. He'd heard enough. He knew the situation spinning out of control around the world meant only one thing, his mission would have to succeed. The world, even though it didn't know it, needed him to succeed. Millions, if not billions of lives depended upon his securing the object.

He'd finished stuffing away his equipment into his pack. He looked out the flap of his tent to see the wind and snow was still howling around him. Visibility was only a few feet.

Time was of the essence, but he couldn't risk going out in this storm, at least not in the dark. It would be too easy to get oneself killed. No he'd have to wait until dawn. At least then, the sunlight would help guide his way.

## Disappointment Cleaver, May 5th, 5:45 a.m.

The sun was just starting to come up in the east. Long fingers of pink and orange light were sticking up on the horizon. The dark that had enveloped the tent for the past ten hours where Cole and his patient spent the night was slowly beginning to fade.

Cole began to stir and blink his eyes in the building light. At first, he was a bit disoriented, unsure of where he was. His body felt stiff and sore, like he had slept in a single rigid position all night. Cole shook his head to clear the cobwebs and hit something hard, rock like.

"Ow," came a woman's voice.

Cole's memory of the avalanche, his search and recovery of a single victim came back in a flash. Cole immediately became reaware of the fact that he was sharing a sleeping bag with a beautiful woman.

The woman began to stir, reaching up with her hand to rub the spot where she and Cole had hit heads.

Cole was face to face with the woman. He could feel her breath on his checks, see her eyes moving under her eyelids, and feel the warmth of her body, even through all their clothes. These were good signs, very good signs. She had survived the night, and unless she had some unforeseen frost bite or broken bones, she would likely come through the avalanche unscathed.

The woman slowly began to blink her eyes. She was waking up. It was too late for Cole to try and scramble out of the bag. His sleeping bag mate would be wide awake in a matter of moments.

She continued to blink her eyes, almost as if her body was fighting for a just a few more moments of sleep. Yet, she eventually opened them completely.

*This was it.* Cole thought.

The woman had beautiful green eyes, like something one would see on a Hollywood actress. They were deep and captivating.

Cole could see that despite her eyes being almost completely open, she wasn't fully awake. A look of sleep or drowsiness still covered her face.

"Hello," she said in a low voice.

"Ah, hello," Cole answered.

"How are you?" she asked. Closing her eyes again and moving her head in closer to Cole's. She pulled the sleeping bag up over her cheeks and snuggled in close to the ranger.

"It's cold," she went on in a voice that was muffled by the sleeping bag. "Hold me tighter."

"Ah, okay," Cole stammered. He wasn't sure how to react. He'd never woken up with a hypothermic patient while sharing the same sleeping bag. *What was the acceptable medical protocol here?* He wondered. Cole decided he'd better tell his patient her current condition.

"How are you feeling?" Cole started.

"Cold," came the one word drowsy response.

Cole started to wiggle his way out of the bag.

"That's making it worse," the woman complained. Her eyes blinking open once more.

Cole and the woman made eye contact again. A sleepy smile built on her face, but this time something was different Cole could see. His patient's eyes were starting to clear; it was obvious her faculties were returning to her.

Then almost is if she was hit by lighting, a flash of awareness, mixed with panic shot across her face.

"Who the fuck are you?" she yelled. The woman started thrashing, trying to escape the hold of the sleeping bag. "Get the fuck off me!"

Cole did everything he could to accommodate the woman's demands. Her violent thrusts and kicks would leave lasting marks on the ranger's body. He protected his head and neck the best he could, while turning his more "sensitive" areas from her flaying kicks.

The two rolled around the tiny tent, still stuck together by the sleeping bag. Neither Cole nor the woman were able to free themselves from their down filled trap. From outside the tent, the kicking and screaming were drowned out by the continuing wind. Inside, their wriggling and writhing made the sleeping bag look like a giant earthworm squirming on a hook.

Cole realized they weren't going to get out if they continued to fight, at least not before both were bruised and exhausted.

"Hold on!" he commanded in his best police voice. "I'm a park ranger and pulled you from the avalanche!"

At that the woman stopped fighting. Cole could see the mention of the avalanche had triggered something in her, some recognition of her accident.

"Avalanche…" the woman whispered. "That's right, I was hit by an avalanche." She rubbed her head for what seemed like quite a while. "My head hurts," she finally said.

"I would think so," Cole reassured the woman. "You got hit by quite a snow slide. You're lucky to be alive."

The woman looked around the tent, "Where am I?"

"We are in a tent, still up on the mountain. I was able to pull you from the slide but not able to get you off the mountain before the storm hit," Cole explained. "What's your name?"

"Aimee," the woman said. "Aimee Crocker."

"Well Ms. Crocker you are one lucky woman. The slide you got swept up in was one of the largest I've ever seen and dare say maybe one of the largest in the mountain's history. The debris field stretches at least a mile down the mountain slope."

Cole could see the woman was still trying to wrap her head around the situation.

"Why are we sharing a sleeping bag?" Crocker asked.

"You were extremely hypothermic. I had to get your body temperature up quickly. I'd heard that body contact was a last ditch way to treat severe cases like yours."

"You didn't take my clothes off did you?" the woman asked with panic rising in her voice. She lifted up the sleeping bag opening, to reveal no state of undress.

149

"No, no, nothing like that occurred, I promise" Cole stammered, obviously embarrassed by the question.

Crocker lowered the bag over her body again. It was apparent nothing torrid had occurred while she was out. Crocker smoothed the bag out over her body once more, almost as if she was making the bed of royalty.

"Why not?" she asked, with a slight rise in one eyebrow. "You don't like girls?"

"What? No. I mean yes, of course I like girls," Cole protested. "huh?"

"Just curious, a good looking guy like you. It would be a shame if you played for the other team."

Cole was suddenly aware of how cramped and hot the little tent had become. "Look I'm flattered," he continued "but you aren't entirely out of the woods here," Cole let her pun go unacknowledged. "Can you tell me anything more about the avalanche? Did you have any other climbing partners that we should be looking for?"

At that, an obvious flash of panic spread across Crocker's face and body. It was as if terror had physically grabbed ahold of her. She started a frantic scramble out of the sleeping bag.

"I've got to get out of here," she cried, her voice shaken with fear.

"Wait!" Cole commanded. "Where do you think you're going?"

"Away from here," Crocker answered. "Far away from here."

"Why, we're perfectly safe here? In fact, it's NOT safe to head out yet with the storm still raging."

The wind picked up again and shook the tent violently. While the dark was lifting, it was apparent the storm was still packing a punch.

"It would be suicide to go out in these conditions," Cole warned.

"It will be suicide to stay here," Crocker countered.

"Why? What the hell is going on?" Cole challenged, his voice rising in anger.

Crocker climbed out of the sleeping bag, zipped up her jacket, and adjusted her hat. She pulled on her goggles and gloves. "I'm going, you can come with me or stay here. Either way I don't care."

Cole could see that Crocker's mind was made up. There was no stopping her. It was against his better judgement, but he decided to go with her. It was better to go with her now and keep her out of trouble, than have to head out later and rescue her once again.

"Hold your horses," Cole commanded. "I'm coming with you. However, before we head out you need to tell me what the hell is going on."

Crocker tied her boots and took a deep breath. "Alright, but it will have to be quick. We likely don't have much time."

## Below Disappointment Cleaver, May 5th, 5:45 a.m.

The Tall Man had been climbing up the avalanche chute for more than an hour. He believed he was just about in the same location where he'd first been swept down the mountain. It had been a long climb. During it, the Tall Man realized his fall down the mountain had been harder on him that he first understood. His body ached and he'd become aware of a bump on his head.

The climb was nearly straight up, a staircase with three foot tall steps, stretching onto infinity. On several occasions, the Tall Man had to catch his balance. The steep ascent and the increase in altitude gained with every step made the climb extremely difficult. He'd caught his step several times, but had always avoided a catastrophic slip and fall. He was tired, but had to push on.

A couple times he dodged wagon wheel sized boulders that tumbled down the mountain. If he'd been struck by one of these rolling monsters, it would be game over. If he wasn't killed outright, the blunt force trauma from the impact and likely fall would eventually do him in.

His slow but steady climb also revealed the snow field he traversed to be unstable. He had inadvertently caused a few minor snow slides, reminding him that the mountain still had the power to sweep him to oblivion.

As if that wasn't enough, he was certain that he felt at least one earthquake while making his climb. It was a small one, but still an earthquake all the same. Earth's movement had set loose its own cascade of rock and snow, causing the Tall Man to curse, "what more could go wrong."

When this mission was over, he'd head to the Caribbean for some much needed R and R. He'd earned it and when he buttoned up this current mess he will have deserved it even more.

That would not come shortly, right now he had to focus on the task at hand. He had to tie up some loose ends. Not the least of which was silencing Crocker. She had learned too much, but she didn't know everything. She was close to learning the ultimate truth and if she did, the Tall Man couldn't trust her to keep the truth secret. No she'd likely tell the world the truth and cast humanity's future into doubt.

He couldn't let that happen, he'd have to succeed no matter how many people had to be killed.

The Tall Man didn't enjoy taking innocent life, but what was the alternative? He'd "volunteered" for this position, for this job. Actually, though, he didn't have much choice. When he signed up all those years ago, he'd been told he'd be protecting the United States' security, but it quickly became apparent the job was much bigger than national security. The world's future actually hung in the balance.

His mission and the agency he worked for enjoyed the highest secrecy. The Tall Man was told the secrecy surpassed even the famed Manhattan Project, the U.S. government's efforts to build the atomic bomb. Only a select handful of people on the planet knew of its existence. It was such a well-guarded secret that none of the world's leaders were in the loop, including the President of the United States.

The fact that the President was out of the loop had stunned the Tall Man when he first learned this fact. However, it wasn't unprecedented for the commander in chief to not be in the know of a highly classified program, and keeping the president in the dark happened far more often that the public could scarcely imagine. The Iran Contra scandal had been a rouge project in the Reagan White House that had run, apparently, right under the Gipper's nose.

But Iran/Contra had been an illegal operation. The Tall Man was convinced he was involved in a legal operation and there was precedent for cutting the President out of legal missions as well. Plausible deniability if things went south being the primary reasons. Presidents such as FDR were cut from the

Need to Know lists in order to speed response times. Harry Truman, arguably the second most powerful man in United States at the end of World War II, only learned about the Manhattan Project after he ascended to the White House at the death of Roosevelt.

The Tall Man's mission improved its efficiency without executive knowledge. However, that wasn't the primary reason for the secrecy. Rather its success and the ultimate fate of the world depended upon none of the world's leaders knowing of its reality. Oh sure, they may have heard rumors of the operation, but the operation was so fanciful that no serious person outside of Tall Man's team entertained the notion of it actually being operational.

No one except the Crocker family that is. Captain Crocker and now his daughter Aimee Crocker had become the greatest threat to world security. Captain Crocker had stumbled upon the truth behind the Tall Man's mission and was likely to blow the lid off the entire operation. Thankfully, Captain Crocker met with an accident before he could do any real damage. Yet, the Tall Man hadn't anticipated how Aimee Crocker would pick up where her father had left off. She had taken to the search with even more drive and passion than her misguided dad. Even worse, she was closer to revealing the secret than even she knew. The Tall Man was under no illusion that Crocker would keep her mouth shut once she realized the entire scope of the secret the Tall Man was sworn to protect. In the end, the ramification and revelation would likely shake Crocker to her core. Her father died for nothing.

The Tall Man paused after one particularly large step. He was taxing his reserves and needed to find the object soon. The sun was just beginning to peak up over the eastern horizon and he knew with the sun came rising temperatures. Rising temperatures meant the snow would melt and soften, making climbing even more deadly.

He shifted his weight from one foot to another and he felt a slight shake, followed by a deep rumble. The Tall Man nearly lost his balance, as he realized the mountain was shaking once more. This earthquake was more intense than the previous one he'd felt on the climb up. He could see high up on the mountain, rocks and ice being dislodged from the peak's grip by the shaking. He feared another avalanche but none came. Most of the loose material had fallen down the mountain in the previous cascade. It would be days before there was enough snow again to trigger a new slide.

But something strange did happen. The Tall Man could see that in the same area where bits of rock and ice continued to break off the mountain, a crack appeared to be forming in the glacier. The shaking earth was placing stress and pressure on Mount Rainier's glaciers and the rivers of ice were cracking under the strain. By his estimates, the Tall Man guessed the new crevasse was a half dozen feet wide and a football field long.

*Glad I'm not up there*, the Tall Man thought to himself.

The shaking eventually stopped and the rumbling subsided. Regaining his balance, the Tall Man returned to his task at hand.

He scanned the area. He was certain he was close to the object's last known location, but the avalanche had dramatically change the landscape; the Tall Man was having trouble orienting himself to his location. He was certain an experienced climber, someone who was familiar with the mountain would quickly be able to figure out where he was, but the Tall Man was neither an expert climber and certainly wasn't intimately familiar with Mount Rainier. Oh, he knew of the mountain. Who in his line of work couldn't be aware of this location. It was the site of the first recorded UFO sighting in the country, in the world, as well as the site where the world's most important secret had been buried for more than half a century. Every new agent learned the history of how the object had been lost and if possible, their primary duty was to secure it.

The Tall Man was grateful that he would be the one to recover it. He would soon close the greatest security risk since the Russian's infiltrated the American's Manhattan Project to build the atomic bomb.

He wouldn't succeed if he couldn't figure out where he was. He looked around the ice field. Nothing looked familiar. He continued his survey of the immediate area, an expanse roughly the size of several football fields. Making matters worse, this snowfield was one of countless others that appeared to stretch onto the horizon. He quickly realized he was not looking for a needle in a haystack. He was looking for a needle in a haystack of a thousand haystacks.

Panic and depression were starting to creep in. He might not recovery the object. *"Stop it!"* He ordered himself, pushing those thoughts and feelings from his mind. He'd drive on.

He was beginning his climb again when a tiny pin prick of light just above his current position on the snowfield caught his eye. He pulled out his binoculars and took a closer look.

Through his field glasses high-powered optics he spotted what looked like a small two-man tent. The National Park Service arrowhead logo could easily be made out on its side.  Well that meant the Park

159

Service was in the area. That meant rangers, who had radios, with which they could call for more rangers.

"Shit!" he muttered to himself.

Just then a lone figure shot out of the tent. The Tall Man focused his spy glasses on the person. It was Crocker. She was in a hurry and given her arm waving and head shaking appeared upset about something. She pointed back toward the tent in obvious gesture that the Tall Man believed meant stay there.

The Tall Man swept his binoculars field of vision toward the direction Crocker was pointing. There just emerging from the tent was a Park Ranger. The Tall Man could see the ranger was pleading to Crocker. About what the Tall Man could only guess. However, it seemed the two were in some type of argument.

The Tall Man returned his gaze to Crocker who was waving her arms with even more excitement. Only a blind man could fail to see that Crocker wanted to be left alone. The Tall Man swept his view back to the ranger who was holding up a single finger in a "just a moment" gesture. The ranger ducked back into the tent and in a few short moments reemerged this time holding an ice axe and a coil of climbing rope.

*Good*, the Tall Man thought. They were going on a climb, and the Tall Man was pretty sure he knew where they were going.

## Disappointment Cleaver, May 5th 5:45 a.m.

"I don't want you coming with me!" Crocker yelled at Cole who had just emerged from the tent. "I don't need, nor want your help!"

"Tough luck," Cole responded slinging the rope coil over his head. He tucked his head and right arm through the loop so that the rope hung over his left shoulder and down toward his waist like a bandolier.

"Look, I don't care what you do. You obviously have something important to do given your panic to get going so quickly. However, I'd be on the hook if I let you walk off a cliff or fall into a crevasse."

Crocker dismissed Cole's concern with a wave of her hand and a roll of the eyes.

"If you want to kill yourself that's your business," Cole went on undeterred, "but like I said it will be my ass in hot water if you get yourself killed on this mountain." Cole's voice now took on a joking tone, "Besides. there's a lot of paperwork that goes into an accident report and I'd just like to avoid the whole process if possible."

Cole could see that Crocker realized he wouldn't be chased off so easily. It became apparent, he was going with her.

"Fine, suit yourself," she muttered in reservation.

"Fine," Cole mimicked. "Are you now going to tell me where we are headed and why we have to leave so quickly?"

"I'm not telling you shit," Crocker stated without even looking back.

"Well then it's going to be a quiet walk. I thought we could use the time to get to know each other," Cole offered.

Crocker didn't take the suggestion. The two headed off in silence.

After a while, Cole broke the stillness. "So where are your climbing buddies?"

"What?" Crocker asked.

"Your climbing buddies? The people you came up here with. Aren't you worried about them?" Cole prodded.

"I don't have any climbing buddies," Crocker asserted. "I'm up here on my own."

"That's odd," Cole said with his eyes slighted squinted. "Then I wonder who those people are pictured on your camera?"

"You went through my pictures?" Crocker yelled, stopping dead in her tracks. "You have no right to access those images! It's a violation of my fourth amendment rights."

"Well given that you were unconscious and in need of immediate medical attention, I took a look at your pictures to see if it might tell me who you are."

"As soon as we get back to civilization, I'll sue you!"

"Go ahead, I'll take my chances with the judge. I'm sure she'd love to hear how everyone you came up here with ended up dead."

Crocker pointed her finger directly at Cole and started to lecture the ranger on the law, and her right to be here and on and on.

Cole cut her off. He moved ahead of Crocker cutting off her forward climb. "Enough! I'd hoped by entertaining your little jaunt here that you'd take the opportunity to tell me about your colleagues, but it's obvious you're not going to do that. So, rather than doing this the easy way, its looks like we will have to do it the hard way."

Cole reached behind his back for his handcuffs. "Ms. Crocker I'm sorry to tell you this, but I can't let you go any farther. I'm placing you under arrest."

Cole moved closer to Crocker but was stopped by a low, deep rumble. Then the ground began to shake, imperceptibly at first, but building until it grew violent. The shaking knocked both Cole and Crocker to the ground.

The two scrambled to regain their feet, but the shaking became more intense, the rumbling more deafening. Crocker lay prone on the ice a few yards from Cole. He too was flat on his stomach.

A loud crack could be heard, like the sound of the world's largest tree breaking in half. But it wasn't a tree being torn apart, it was the ice upon which Crocker and Cole lay that was splitting. The crack started high upon the mountain, but spread quickly down the slope and cut between the downed climbers. The crack continued down the glacier like a giant snake.

Neither Crocker nor Cole could regain their feet. They held on for dear life like a rodeo cowboy on a bull.

The crevasse began to spread threatening to suck in the two. Cole being farther away from the chasm was able to scramble to safety. Crocker wasn't so lucky. The crack had formed virtually under her and the crevasse spread faster than her ability to crawl away. Before she could really even assess what was going on, Crocker toppled head first into the chasm.

Almost on cue, the shaking stopped. It appeared the earthquake was over. Cole scrambled to his feet as quickly as he could and raced to the edge of the crevasse, expecting to find Crocker had vanished into the depths of the river of ice.

But to his relief, she had not disappeared. Rather, her fall had been broken by an ice shelf, roughly 15 feet below. She lay motionless on the tiny ledge. Cole feared she might be unconscious or worse.

He called down to her. "Crocker! Can you hear me?"

Nothing. Crocker's body lay lifeless.

Cole recovered his binoculars from his pack and zoomed in on Crocker's face, hoping to make out a hint of life. Through the cascade of snow that continued to fall into the crevasse, Cole could make out wisps of steam rising from Crocker's nostrils. She was alive, but for how much longer, he couldn't be sure.

*Thank God*, Cole thought to himself.

Cole got on his radio and called in his situation.

"Paradise? This is Cole! I've got an emergency. Over!"

Beth's young, but reassuring, voice came back through the walkie-talkie speaker almost immediately.

"What's up boss? You alright?"

"Yes, I'm fine," Cole responded. "A little shaken up by the earthquake," Cole said sarcastically. "However, I've got a climber who has fallen into a crevasse. She appears unconscious."

"Roger," came back the reply.

"I'm going to attempt a rescue, however I'll need a helicopter Evac ASAP! I'm concerned the victim may have broken some limbs and perhaps even internal injuries."

"Copy that," Beth replied. "I'll call mercy flight rescue team!"

"What? Where is the Army helicopter out of Fort Lewis? They're closer by nearly 30 minutes!"

"Oh, that's right you don't know," Beth began.

"I don't know what?"

"That the President has placed all military personnel, bases, and its aircraft on full alert, on account of the building crisis between the US and Russia," she answered. "The helicopters at Fort Lewis simply aren't available."

"Great," Cole cursed. "Okay, put the call into Mercy Flight, but urge them to step on it."

"Will do," Beth answered.

The radio went silent. Cole likely had an hour before the helicopter was on scene. He'd have plenty of time to get Crocker out of the hole, provide a first response to any obvious injuries, and stabilize her for transport.

Cole dropped the coil of rope he'd been carrying and began to lay it out on the snow. He made certain to prevent the rope from bunching up into knots or tangles. He created a rope anchoring point by digging a deep tear dropped shaped trench into the snow and ice with Crocker's dropped ice axe. He laced the rope through the trench, securing the up mountain end with a knot.

He dropped the other end of the rope into the crevasse, making sure to not hit the prone Crocker. Cole secured his self-arresting belay pulley to the rope and snapped it to his climbing harness. He placed his back to the crevasse and began slowly backing up toward the crack. At its edge, he took one foot and kicked the prongs of his crampon into the ice wall. He shifted his weight to onto this foot and kicked his other foot into the ice, a little lower than his first kick-in spot. He repeated this process, slowly inching his way down the wall. Intermittently he called out to Crocker. Still no response.

Cole lowered himself down to Crocker's level and did a quick assessment of her. She didn't appear to have any apparent fractures or bleeding wounds. That was good news, but he really wouldn't be able to learn her situation until he got her up to the surface.

Thankfully, she wasn't wedged into the crevasse. The small ledge held Crocker up, keeping her from falling deeper into the abyss. Cole believed he had enough rope to get her out, but if she had gone deeper or been stuck, he wasn't sure he'd be able to pull her out.

Cole checked Crocker's climbing gear. Thankfully, her climbing harness was still attached. The ranger snapped two weight bearing carabiners to her belt and secured them to the rope with a follow through figure eight knot.

He pulled on the rope, testing the knot and carabiner to make sure it would hold Crocker's weight. Satisfied with their strength, he started to climb back up to the surface. Cole pulled himself up on top of the ice. He dug a small trench under the rope and placed his avalanche shovel in the trench and under the rope. This would prevent the rope from disappearing into the snow. To prevent the shovel from being pulled into the crevasse, he secured the handle of the shovel to the ice with Crocker's ice axe. Cole built a Z pulley system which would allow him to climb up the mountain and pull Crocker out of her trap.

Cole kicked in and began the effort to extract Crocker. The rope pulled tight as Cole began to lift his victim. The lift was slow and difficult, but ever so slightly Cole moved Crocker closer and closer to the surface. He continued to pull, Crocker's limp body continued to rise. Eventually, her body reached the surface. Cole pulled her over the edge and dragged her limp figure a safe distance onto the ice. The last thing Cole wanted was for Crocker to slip back into the crevasse.

Once Crocker was safely out of danger, Cole secured the rope holding his victim. He detached himself from the line and quickly returned to Crocker's side.

Crocker was breathing, although her respiration was labored. She had taken a bad fall. He scanned her from head to toe, feeling for lumps and deformities that could indicate broken bones or internal bleeding. She appeared to be okay, but Cole couldn't be certain until Crocker was examined by a doctor, and that wouldn't happen until the Mercy Helicopter had picked them up and transported them to a nearby hospital.

Cole scanned the sky searching for the helicopter. Nothing was visible yet. He checked his watch, the Mercy Flight would likely be here in ten to fifteen minutes. Cole felt certain that Crocker was stable, at least for now. He immediately began to search the area for a suitable helicopter landing area.

He needed the landing zone to be a level piece of ice, one that was a fair distance from the current crevasse. *God help us,* he thought if the helicopter went down because it fell into the hole he'd just pulled Crocker out of. "The day had gone from bad to worse," he muttered, "let's make sure it doesn't go from worse to disaster."

In the distance, over the blowing wind, Cole began to make out the faint "whomp, whomp, whomp" of an approaching helicopter. It had to be the rescue chopper.

Just a few dozen yards from where Crocker lay on the ice, Cole found a suitable landing site. It was clear of any large boulders and ice chunks. Cole grabbed a smoke grenade from his backpack and waited for the aircraft to come into view.

"Ranger Cole," came a female voice over the ranger's radio. "This is Mercy Flight Tango Sierra inbound to your position. Do you copy? Over."

"Mercy Flight, this is Ranger Cole. I copy you loud and clear."

"Excellent, we are approximately 60 seconds from your position. Do you have a suitable landing site identified?"

"Affirmative," Cole replied. "I'm about to mark the site with a smoke grenade and will guide you in."

"Roger."

"Be advised," Cole looked around before he went on. "Visibility is approximately 3 miles with slight winds, perhaps 5 knots out of the south. I'd advise you approach from the North, with the mountain on your right side."

"Copy. We are 30 second out."

Cole pulled the pin on the smoke grenade and placed it uphill of the landing zone. A large cloud began billowing out of the device. The cloud bent slightly and traveled in a northerly direction, just as Cole had reported.

"Ranger Cole, this is Mercy Flight we have green smoke just south of Disappointment Cleaver. Is that your signal?"

"Affirmative."

"Perfect."

Cole could hear the whomp, whomp, whomp of the rotors. The engine noise was getting louder, but he still had not made visual contact with the craft.

Just then the BK 117 Mercy Flight crested a nearby rise. Cole could easily make out the orange and blue paint scheme and could see the sunglass wearing pilots inside the domed canopy. He began to wave his arms in order to get the pilots' attention. The pilot apparently spotted Cole, and began a slow descent to the landing zone. Cole cleared out of the way. He retrieved the smoke grenade and shut it down.

The helicopter hovered for a moment above the ice, Cole guessed the pilot was making a final check of the site or judging the wind before committing her craft to the landing. However, after a brief few seconds, the craft finally set down. The two pilots shut down the engines and the rotors gently spun to a halt. Two, what Cole assumed were EMT's, bounded from the craft, heading toward him.

He waved them to follow and led them to where he'd left Crocker. She was still out cold on the ice. The EMTs set their medical gear down next to the patient and began to assess her immediate condition. Cole gave them an overview of what he believed was her condition.

The EMTs grabbed a blood pressure cuff, stethoscopes and other medical devices from their bags. One retrieved a small oxygen bottle from her bag. A mask and hose were attached to the bottle. She placed the mask over Crocker's mouth and nose, and began the oxygen flow.

Almost immediately, Crocker began to respond. She fluttered her eyes and slowly moved her head.

"Easy," one the EMT said. "Can you hear me?"

Crocker seemed to hear the question and murmured a reply.

The EMT looked to Cole, pointed to Crocker and asked, "What's her name?"

"Aimee Crocker."

"Amiee? Can you hear me?" the EMT asked.

"Yes, I can hear you." Crocker replied in a still low voice.

"That's good. Are you in pain?"

Crocker seemed to contemplate the question for a second, took a deep breath and answered, "no," in a quiet voice, "although, I'm not sure what happened?"

"Understandable," the EMT replied. "Do you know who you are? Where you are? What day it is?"

"I'm Amiee Crocker. I'm on Mount Rainier and its May 5th."

"Great, it seems your memory hasn't been affected. That's good news. However, to be safe we are taking you to the hospital. There may be internal injuries that we can better spot and treat in a medical facility."

Cole could see that Crocker was contemplating an objection, but seemed to think better of it. "Okay," she conceded.

"Excellent, let me get the stretcher and we will get you loaded up."

The female EMT returned to the helicopter and retrieved the medevac stretcher. It wasn't the typical metal basket type litter. Rather, Cole thought the stretcher resembled something like a large vampire cape made of high strength polypropylene material.

The stretcher was spread out on the snow next to Crocker. The first EMT gently placed a cervical collar around Crocker's neck, immobilizing it from any further harm. Next Cole and the two EMT's carefully lifted Crocker onto it. Belts and straps were used to encase Crocker and secure her from falling out of the litter. Cole marveled at the ingenious design which gave the patient a feeling of security, but was light weight and could be rolled up to fit within a midsized backpack. *Pretty cool* he thought.

Once the lead EMT was certain Crocker was comfortable and secure in the orange stretcher, the three rescuers lifted her and transported the patient to the waiting helicopter.

The helicopters' pilots were beginning the preflight checklist, as the two EMT's slid Crocker into place. They secured additional straps across her chest locking the litter onto the copter's floor. It wasn't going anywhere.

The engine began to wind up with a sound that reminded Cole of a zipper. The ranger took one last look around the accident site. He scanned the new crevasse and made a mental note that he'd have to alert his climbing rangers to the new obstacles. He was also glad he wouldn't have to walk back down the mountain. The crevasse was between him and his destination and by his rough estimate it was too big for him to cross alone.

The helicopter engines were running at full speed now. Cole climbed into the passenger compartment right next to Crocker and closed the copter's side door.

The cabin was heating up nicely and it promised to be a nice smooth, albeit short, ride to the nearby Eatonville hospital.

Cole and the other passengers strapped on headphones to protect their ears. Through its speakers, Cole heard the pilot request a priority and immediate departure from Mount Rainier. The FAA air traffic control granted the request while providing flight vectors, weather, and nearby traffic information.

The pilot thanked ATC and turned toward the passenger cabin, "Hold on, we are going to lift off."

Cole and the others secured their seatbelts and prepared for their assent.

At that the engine began to throttle up, the rotors spinning faster and faster. The helicopter slowly lifted from its icy perch, taking what felt like a tentative hop off the ice. Cole imagined it was what a young eagle or hawk felt like when they made their first attempt to fly the nest.

After one more pre take-off hop, the helicopter eventually lifted off the snow and ice and rose like an elevator into the air. Cole, from his door side seat, had a panoramic view of the surrounding area. The helicopter rose higher, increasing the visible landscape outside the window.

Cole could see the crevasse stretching far down the glacier, at least a hundred yards if not more. He'd estimated correctly that where he'd pulled Crocker from the ice, the gap was more than 6 feet across. In other places the crack was even wider. Cole scanned the crevasse from one end to the other. It resembled a long and nasty scar on the otherwise dirty, snow white glacier.

The helicopter leveled off at what Cole guessed was about 100 ft above the glacier and began to accelerate forward. He could now see the entire length of the crevasse, including sections that had been hidden to him when he was on the surface. In the distance and its far end, Cole spotted an unusual object. It appeared to be something similar to a black pyramid or witches hat half buried in a snowbank. Cole grabbed his binoculars and zoomed in on it. However, to his frustration he had difficultly focusing his field glasses on the object. It was as if the object was enveloped in something similar to a mirage. It was both there and not. Cole couldn't quite understand what he was seeing, but he was sure it wasn't a natural object like volcanic glass.

Perhaps it was an experimental aircraft or some type of military marker like a navigation beacon. But that couldn't be it. Although, Cole wasn't privy to all military matters that took place in his park, it was customary for the Department of Defense to give him a heads up of any equipment that was to be placed within park boundaries. If for no other reason, Park Rangers tended to know their parks extremely well and could help military personnel site their equipment to achieve their goals, while maximizing safety and minimizing resource damage. It didn't always work. And sometimes the military purposely cut the park service out of the loop. Which is what appeared to be the case here. He made a mental note to contact his Army liaison the following week at nearby Fort Lewis and try to get an explanation of what he'd found. The marker or whatever it was, was adjacent to a popular climbing route and it was only a matter of time before someone found and eventually messed with it. Cole hoped his talking with his Army colleagues would prevent the need for the military to issue denials or worse, the Park Service's having to partake in a fabricated cover story.

Cole put down his binoculars and began to settle back into his seat. Above the noise of the rotors and the shaking of the aircraft Cole thought he heard and felt three thumps coming from its engine compartment.

Then all hell broke loose.

## Disappointment Cleaver, May 5th 5:45 a.m.

The Tall Man watched and followed Crocker and the ranger as they left their tent. He'd considered taking both them out right then, but he still hadn't found the object and by the look of it, he felt the two knew where they were going. If not, he'd follow them for a while and make his move when he felt it appropriate.

He could see that Crocker appeared to be on a mission, as if she was heading toward something. Or perhaps, he considered, away from something. He hoped it was the former but understood if it was the latter.

The Tall Man checked his watch. He wasn't sure how long he'd let the two go, but it wouldn't be forever. He cursed losing his rifle, but there was nothing he could do about that now. He'd have to make do with the tools he had. Besides this wasn't his first mission when he went in with less than the necessary tools. He'd been sent out into the field many times with little more than the clothes on his back and always succeeded.

Yet this mission felt different. He'd never confronted such a committed adversary. Crocker was on a mission, motivated not by greed or some hatred of the federal government. Rather she was pushed forward by a more powerful force, a wish to redeem her father. That type of motivation is not easily pushed off the trail.

The Tall Man had to respect Crocker's determination, but the end would be the same. Crocker like her climbing partners, and now this ranger, wouldn't see tomorrow. He checked his pistol. It was fully loaded with a 15 round clip.

He was roughly 100 yards behind his prey. He felt he could hit them from this distance, but he had to make certain. He'd have to get closer. He'd wait for a better opportunity.

At that, the ground started to shake. *Another fucking earthquake!* he thought. The Tall Man got to the ground and did his best to hold on, but this time, the shaking passed fairly quickly. There was no avalanche, no crashing boulders. He counted himself lucky. He quickly realized his prey was in trouble. Perhaps fate would take care of them for him. Crocker had fallen into a crevasse and that likely would serve as her tomb.

However, the Tall Man watched as the ranger pulled Crocker from the abyss. The Tall Man thought about killing them while they were vulnerable. Yet, through the binoculars it was obvious the ranger had called for help. The mountain would soon be buzzing with people. The Tall Man could likely kill the ranger, but he wasn't certain of Crocker's condition or position.

He wasn't sure he could get to her before help arrived. Moreover, if the expected rangers found to dead bodies with bullet holes in their bodies, that would only lead to more questions and ultimately more people scrambling around the object. He'd have to reconsider his options. He'd have to come up with a new plan on the fly.

He watched the ranger for the next thirty minutes, he watched him descend into the crack, reemerge several minutes later, set up a pulley system and eventually pull Crocker to surface, just as a helicopter stared to come in from the north. *This ranger was one lucky guy, there hadn't been enough time for the Tall Man to sneak up and possibly trap both in the crevasse.*

The Tall Man watched as the helicopter landed, powered down and two paramedics leaped from its cabin. They set upon Crocker and assessed the situation. With the ranger's help they secured her to a stretcher and prepared to move to the copter.

The Tall Man could see everyone was fixated on the task at hand, including the pilots. He decided to make his move. He slowly and carefully moved his way closer toward the rescue party, making certain he remained out of sight of his prey.

Within the time it had taken the paramedics to secure Crocker to the stretcher, transport her to the helicopter, he was close enough to hear their conversation. By the time the copter's twin engines fired up, he could make out their facial features. *Close enough,* he decided.

He wanted to make sure he brought down the helicopter in such a way that it appeared to be an accident and maximize the chance that all on board would be killed. He watched as the machine tentatively lifted up off the ice and ascended into the sky.

He continued to watch it rise straight up. He pulled his pistol from its holster and took aim at the helicopter's engine compartment. When it reached a height of about a tall tree, he pulled the trigger and put three bullets into it.

## Helicopter over Disappointment Cleaver, May 5th 6:15 a.m.

Alarms and warning sirens filled the helicopter's passenger cabin. The copter began to buck and bounce, the engine started to sputter. Cole could see out the window the cloud of black smoke pouring from the engine compartment.

"Well, that's not good," Cole said sarcastically.

"MAYDAY! MAYDAY! MAYDAY!" Cole heard the pilot call over the headphones. Meanwhile, the pilot and copilot frantically flipped switches, pulled levers, and wrestled with the flight stick in a losing battle to maintain control of their craft.

The pilot turned her head and addressed her passengers, "Brace yourself! We're going down!"

The helicopter continued its violent fall from the sky. The two pilots heroically did their best to keep the craft airborne, but nothing they did seemed to work. The helicopter now began too spiral in a clock ward motion. The world outside the helicopter's windows began to whirl faster and faster.

Cole and the rest of the passengers checked their seatbelts. The paramedics onboard immediately got into a brace position. They obviously had been either trained for this scenario or crashed before. Either way, Cole followed suit and prepared as best he could for the impact.

The two pilots continued their futile struggle to keep their craft airborne, but eventually the laws of physics won out. The helicopter pitched slightly to the left, while the pilots struggled to keep it level. In doing so, they over compensated and the doomed craft's sputtering rotors struck the ground. A sickening screech of twisting and buckling metal filled the cabin. All aboard instinctively ducked their head in anticipation of bits and pieces of broken metal violently spinning off in every direction. Milliseconds later the cabin and flight deck were riddled with bullet like projectiles of what just seconds before had been the rotors. The two paramedics were cut down immediately. Cole and Crocker were splattered with their blood.

The helicopter's fuselage struck the ground next in an equally violent fashion. It went into the rock hard side of Mount Rainier in a slight left leaning nose down fashion. The entire right front of the helicopter collapsed in the impact, crushing the pilot. The co-pilot's seatbelt restraints failed and flung him through what remained of the windshield.

The helicopter, despite smacking the side of the mountain, continued its leftward spin resulting in a roll that ended with the craft coming to rest upside down.

Just as quickly as it had started, the crash was over. The cabin was surprisingly quiet, except for the crackling and popping fire that was rapidly engulfing the helicopter's engine compartment. Cole was hanging upside down in the cabin. Unlike the co-pilot's seatbelt, Cole's had held and was holding him in his seat. He did a quick assessment of his physical condition. Nothing seemed out of the ordinary. He didn't discover or believe he'd suffered any major injuries. However, that would change if he didn't get out of the downed helicopter and soon.

Cole found Crocker still securely strapped into her stretcher. The stretcher itself was firmly secured to its tie downs. Cole quickly assessed Crocker's condition. She too appeared no worse for the wear, she was breathing. He then turned his attention to the two paramedics. Unfortunately, they weren't so lucky. Both were peppered from head to toe with countless punctures and gapping wounds that in both cases were obviously fatal.

Cole looked to the pilot and co-pilot. The pilot as well was obviously dead. The co-pilot was missing and apparently had been ejected from the vehicle.

The engine fire continued to grow and smoke now fully engulfed the helicopter cabin. It was time to abandon ship. Hanging upside down, made it extremely difficult to secure the seatbelts release. He struggled for a few seconds with the belt buckle, it wouldn't release. Cole gave up and grabbed a Swiss army knife from his pocket and cut himself free of his seatbelt. Cutting the four restraints, resulted in his falling like a sack of laundry to the roof of the craft.

Cole turned to Crocker who was still strapped to the stretcher; however she was slowly coming out of the daze from her fall in the crevasse. "What the hell is going on?" she asked as she hung above Cole.

"The helicopter crashed, and we've got to get out of here. And fast."

"This is one hell of a day and rescue. First I wake up in a sleeping bag with you, and then I'm told I hit my head falling into a crevasse, now I'm in a helicopter crash. What's next? Being dragged off by bigfoot?"

"Not likely. Everyone knows Bigfoot lives in the lowlands," Cole joked. "This is abominable snowman habitat."

That got a smile and a muted chuckle out of Crocker.

"Okay, I was wrong," Cole admitted.

"What?" Crocked questioned.

"You do have teeth," Cole joked some more. "I thought perhaps the reason you didn't smile was that you'd had your teeth knocked out playing hockey or something."

"No I didn't have my teeth knocked out playing hockey," Crocker began. "However, I will neither confirm nor deny whether I've knocked out people's teeth playing the sport."

"Fair enough," Cole surrendered with a smile.

The fire and smoke began to build in the cabin making it extremely hard to see and breathe.

"Perhaps we should continue this conversation elsewhere," Cole offered.

"Agreed," Crocker decided.

Cole took his pocket knife and cut Crocker free from her restraints. He made certain to do so slowly and carefully making sure that she wouldn't fall to the cabin ceiling like he'd done. She'd had enough falling for one day.

Once free, the two kicked open the helicopter's side door. Cole grabbed his backpack and the two crawled clear of the wreckage. The fire had now fully engulfed the craft, sending an inkuy, stinking black column of smoke high into the air.

A couple things became obvious as the two watched the machine burn. The helicopter wouldn't provide any shelter from the elements. It would soon be reduced to nothing more than a burnt husk, little more than charred rubble of metal and melted plastic. Next, the building smoke trail would alert the authorities that something was wrong on the mountain. Rangers would be sent to investigate. Unfortunately, the pending storm would mean another rescue wouldn't be attempted until it passed at best. They would have to find shelter and soon. Without some type of protection from the cold, both would likely be dead before the end of the day.

Cole looked around the surroundings. There was nothing but snow and ice as far as the eye could see. Camp Muir was miles away and his little tent was nowhere to be seen. They were stuck and facing a very difficult day.

Crocker stared at the burning helicopter. She turned to Cole and said "Okay, well watching the fire has been fun, but I think we should head to the object before it gets dark."

"Object? What Object?"

Crocker began walking off toward the north, in the direction of the far end of the new crevasse. She stopped, obviously exasperated by the question, "Listen Ranger Rick, I don't know what you think is going on, but there is a big secret here on this mountain."

"What are you talking about?" Cole challenged.

"Look, I like you, you're not a bad looking guy, and although it appears you are a little slow on the up take, I'll let you in on the joke." Crocker began walking again toward her destination. "There is a secret buried on this mountain. It crashed here more than 70 years ago and only recently has been brought to light."

Cole looked around. Seeing that the storm clouds were building and that no one survived the crash, the best course of action was to follow Crocker and hopefully find shelter before the storm hit.

Crocker continued her monologue. "You've heard of Area 51 haven't you?

"Sure, who hasn't?" Cole responded.

"And what do they do there?" Crocker questioned.

"Not entirely sure, but I believe they test aircraft and other advanced technologies." Cole was starting to wonder where this conversation was going.

"Where do you think they get this technology?"

"Again, not entirely sure but the Pentagon has an extremely large budget. I'm sure they contract with businesses and universities to develop their new systems."

"Partially correct," Crocker granted. "The Pentagon definitely has its own research and development program, that's what DARPA is all about."

"DARPA?" Cole asked.

"Sorry, the Defense Advanced Research Projects Agency. Its predecessor was founded in 1958 with a mandate to prevent America from ever being caught again with its pants down from a scientific or technological standpoint."

"Again?"

"Jesus! Do I have to spoon feed you everything?"

Cole let the slight go. He knew his history. He knew about DARPA, the CIA and the federal government's pursuit of advanced technologies. In fact, the Park Service was a beneficiary of some of that that technology including the use of ground penetrating radar and night vision goggles. However, he wanted to keep Crocker talking. He hoped she might shed light on her colleagues. Cole hadn't forgotten that Crocker was hiding something and her climbing buddies were nowhere to be found. He feared they hadn't survived the avalanche, but if this was the case, why wouldn't Crocker tell him? Why had she insisted she had climbed alone?

"Humor me?" he pleaded.

"In 1957, the Soviet Union, a country that was only 12 years removed from the most destructive war in World history, manages to launch the worlds' first artificial satellite into space. American and other world leaders were stunned by this development. It was believed that the USSR was years, if not decades, away from developing ballistic missile technology. Combine this with the Soviet's detonation of an atomic bomb in 1949, and the United States' faced an existential threat."

Crocker marched across the snow, continuing her history lesson. "Congress and the President passed legislation in lightning speed, which created the forerunner to DARPA with a mission to keep the United States forever on the forefront of technological development. America would never again be surprised by the Soviet Union or any other country when it came to advanced military systems."

"Okay, makes sense to me," Cole conceded.

Crocker waited for Cole to ask his next question. He didn't. Exasperated she queued up the unasked request. "Don't you think it odd that since our failure

192

over Sputnik, the United States has been able to consistently stay on the forefront of new technology, always just one step ahead of our enemies? Why do you think this is?"

Cole wasn't sure where Crocker was going with this line of questioning but said "because our scientists and researchers are the best with the biggest budgets?"

"Bullshit!"

"Excuse me?"

"Nope that's not it."

"Okay what is it then?"

"Ever hear of Operation Paper Clip?" Crocker asked.

"Can't say that I have, is it an Office Depot ad campaign?"

"Hardly.

"It was a top secret American military program to secret away high level Nazi scientists out of Germany and back to the U.S. The Americans swooped up German physicists and chemists. They took engineers and munitions experts, but they also got their hands on Wernher Von Braun, a high level Nazi fuck, who just so happened to be the father of the German rocket program."

Cole said nothing.

"So the same guy who built the V2 rockets that rained down terror on London during the last months of the war, also built the rockets that put American's on the moon. What's more, he did it in less than 25 years. In fact, the world hadn't put anything in orbit until the Soviet's launched Sputnik in 1957. So, that means in roughly a dozen years the United States went from no space capable rockets to landing a man on the moon. All with the help of a former Nazi wonder scientist. Coincidence? I don't think so."

Cole blew out a deep breath of air from deep in his lungs. The air instantly froze leaving his mouth, making a huge cloud that engulfed his head. The air was getting colder. It was going to be a cold day. They needed to get under cover and soon. Cole was close to cutting off Crocker and her wild goose chase. If there wasn't some type of shelter on the far side of this ridge, Cole would have to build a snow shelter and fast.

Crocker continued her monologue. "Fast forward to today. The United States is on the cutting edge of drone, stealth, supersonic and other aviation technology. It's been an unprecedented run."

"And you think this is due to what?" Cole asked.

"Do you know where the first documented UFO sighting took place?" Crocker asked.

Cole had a confused look on his face, "Seriously?"

"Yeah," Crocker responded. "Where was the first UFO sighted?"

"Okay, I'll play along. New Mexico right?"

"Wrong," Crocker shot back as she continued her march toward the object. "It was right here, at Mount Rainier National Park."

"What?" Cole questioned.

"You see back in 1947, a private pilot was returning to Montana from a trade show when he spotted 9 disc like objects racing down from Vancouver, Canada, past Mount Rainier, only to disappear over Oregon to the south."

Cole watched Crocker to see if she might be kidding. She wasn't.

"The New Mexico UFO history is better known," Crocker, continued, "in part because a craft reportedly crash there. Initial news reports confirmed the crashed vehicle was a UFO, however military personnel quickly descended upon the Roswell crash site, scooped up the wreckage and changed the official story to a downed weather balloon. Can you believe that crap?"

"No I can't," Cole responded with a slight roll of the eyes.

Cole's sarcastic but skeptical response apparently went over Crocker's head and she continued her history lesson. "So like you, most people don't know the first sighting was here," Crocker swung her arms indicating their general location. However, what people also don't know is that one of the 9 craft also crashed. Care to guess where?"

Cole closed his eyes and shook his head, "Here, on the mountain?"

"That's correct, sport. Give the man a prize," Crocker teased. "One of those craft went down right here on the slopes of Mount Rainier. You want to know one more secret?"

Cole sighed, "Sure I'm in for a penny now might as well put in the entire pound."

"It's still here, just over that ridge." Crocker pointed to the near horizon. "If we move fast, we can get there in about an hour."

"Look lady," Cole began, "It's obvious you hit your head a little harder than I first diagnosed. I can assure you there is no flying saucer on this mountain."

Crocker cut him off, "Wait, I haven't told you the best part yet."

"There's more?"

"Sure there's more! What do you think is going on? Why did you think I was so eager to get out of the tent this morning?"

"Ah, I had morning breath?" Cole joked.

"No," she said sarcastically. "There are others up here looking to prevent my bringing the crash to light."

Now Cole began to question the woman's sanity. "Men in Black, up here on the mountain?" Cole kidded.

"No," Crocker assured and paused for affect. "They're clad in white. What did you think? We are on a snow and ice covered mountain. Their black uniforms would stand out like a sore thumb. What's more they aren't the happy-go-lucky slap stick like people you see in the movies."

"No?" Cole questioned.

"No," Crocker's voice dropped and took on a serious and slightly frightened tone. "They are armed and deadly."

Crocker stopped her march up the mountain and turned to face Cole. "Look," she said emotion filling her voice, "I know you don't believe me. I know you think I'm crazy. But I know there is a crashed UFO on this mountain. I know there are men up here trying to stop me from revealing that fact. I know my father died, was likely killed by these "men in black" because he knew too much about the secret. I know I've lost friends both literally and figuratively in my search for the truth. I'm going to reveal the truth if it's the last think I do. And you will have to kill me to stop my search."

Cole could see the seriousness in Crocker's eyes. Whether any of her story was true or not, Cole didn't know. However, he could see, no he could feel, that Crocker believed it true. The ranger looked around their surroundings. The helicopter was still burning in the distance, while the storm clouds were beginning to slowly slide up over the horizon.

It was going to get cold up here real quick. Unless they found some shelter soon, it wouldn't matter if Crocker's story was true or not. He made a decision. "Okay, Crocker I believe you."

That caught the would-be UFOlologist by surprise. "You do?"

"Sure, I can see how important this is to you. I understand you've made this your life's mission. Who am I to stand in the way of you making the greatest discovery in world history. However?"

"However?" Crocker asked "I knew there was a catch."

"Easy," Cole began, raising a hand in an attempt to calm her concerns. "As I was going to say, however a storm is building and it will be getting cold real quick. We'd better find your UFO and soon or your "men in black" won't have to kill us to keep the secret. We will already be dead. So, lead the way Ms. Crocker."

Crocker looked puzzled. As if she was trying to figure out whether Cole's new support and willingness to help her was some type of trick. Yet she looked around and could see the coming storm. She'd have to trust Cole, just like he'd have to trust her.

"Okay," she said. "It's just over this rise." She pointed to a small ridge, roughly the size of a ten story building. "We will be up and over before the storm is completely on us. "Let's go."

The two began hiking up the hill, placing one foot in front of the other. The air was getting thin up here and Cole could feel the effects of the earthquakes, helicopter crash, and the cold sapping his strength. If the object Crocker was looking for wasn't on the other side of this hill, well he didn't want to think about that.

"Crocker?" Cole asked without waiting for a response. "Mount Rainier is one of the most popular mountains in the country. Thousands of people climb it each year with hundreds taking the very route we are on today. I find it extremely hard to believe an alien space craft has been sitting on its slopes for 70 years and missed by countless people."

"I assume you've heard of the Otzi iceman?" Crocker responded and, like Cole, went on without waiting for a response. "He was a stone age hunter that was killed more than 5,000 years ago. His body lay encased in ice and was only recently discovered, this, despite the fact that Otzi was found in the Alps."

Crocker gave Cole a sideways glance, which Cole believed was her way of seeing if he was paying attention.

"If a man can remain hidden for five millennium in what is possibly the world's most popular mountain range, along a popular hiking route, smack dab in the middle of Europe, it's possible a space craft could be hidden on the slopes of this mountain for a mere five decades."

"I've heard of the Otzi man," Cole sheepishly began. Crocker cut him off with a wave of her hand.

The two continued their climb for another ten minutes in the quiet. Crocker remained in the lead, beating Cole to the top. She stopped at the ridge line. Cole could see her scanning the area below, obviously searching for her prize. Cole continued his one foot in front of the other plod up the snowbank, but kept his gaze locked on his climbing partner. He could see worry spreading across her face. The object wasn't there, he guessed. *Great*! He sarcastically cursed under his breath.

Cole continued his climb, but the concern that was clouding Crocker's face was replaced with joy as the ranger reached the top of the snow bank. She pointed off in the distance and exclaimed, "There it is!"

Cole paused at the top of the berm, and looked in the direction Crocker was indicating. There in the distance was a black triangle type object. It was roughly the size of one story building. It was also the object he'd seen from the helicopter, just before it had crashed. "That's no UFO," Cole began. "It's got to be some type of military navigation beacon or radar system. The military is always dropping this type of equipment in national parks all over the west."

"So, the military told you about this object?" Crocker asked with a surprised tone.

"Well, no," Cole started.

"What? Did the military tell you about this object or not?"

"No," Cole continued, "but the military places these types of objects on public lands all the time, and on several occasions they have failed to tell the land management agency about their actions. You know national security and all."

"Then you actually don't have any idea what that object is, do you?" Crocker challenged.

"When you put it that way," Cole stammered.

"Why don't we go down there and actually look at it before passing judgement on what it is? Okay?"

"Okay."

"I can tell you from personal experience," Crocker stated matter of fact, "it's not a radar installation."

Crocker began the hike down the snow bank. Cole quickly followed. He estimated it would be roughly 10 minutes down the slight incline and another 5 to 10 across the glacier field to the object. Twenty more minutes of hiking. Then he hoped he'd able to tell what this object was, whether they could get shelter nearby and ultimately what might be their chances of surviving the storm.

To pass the time, Cole decided to entertain Crocker's belief about the object.

"Alright, let's just say for the moment I believe that object over there is an alien space craft. What do you know about it?"

"I've been searching for this object almost my entire life. I believe my father had found it or was about to discover it years before. He obviously was close to revealing the truth and for that he was killed."

"Your father?"

"Yes, my father," Crocker explained, "He was in Army intelligence. I remember moving all the time, however a few years before he died, we were detailed for a short period of time at Whitman Air Force Base in Missouri. Do you know Whitman?"

"No, can't say that I do."

"Well it just so happens to be the home of the 509 Operations Group. Have you ever heard of the 509, also sometimes referred to as the Experimental Air Force?"

"Ah, well considering I'd never heard of Whitman I'm going to have to admit I've never heard of the 509 or the Experimental Air Force either."

"Well that doesn't surprise me. Very few have heard of the EAF. It's very hush, hush. However, my father was detailed to Whitman back in the early eighties. His job was to investigate public reports of unexplained aircraft. Any idea which Operations group was called to investigate the New Mexico UFO crash?"

"The 509?" Cole guessed.

"Yes, that's correct. The 509. Kind of odd don't you think that an operations group out of Missouri would be called to investigate a balloon crash in New Mexico? My father joins the 509 and his job just happens to be the investigation of suspicious plane crashes. Back then I used to follow my dad's work very closely. He wasn't aware, but I knew more about what he was doing than he told me."

"Like what?"

"I knew he was unhappy or troubled by something. His mood had changed a few years back and I was convinced his change in temperament had something to do with his work. I'm convinced he uncovered something, perhaps stumbled upon something he shouldn't have and worried about its ramifications. I believe he knew about the Rainier UFO and was set to reveal its existence to the world."

"What makes you think that?"

"Because he killed himself here at Rainier."

Crocker tested the ground in front of her. It appeared a bit unstable. Large cracks could be seen crisscrossing the snow and ice field ahead of the two. Their progress would slow considerably. They would need to rope up or go around the field to reach the object.

Cole looked back and saw a large cloud had cleared the horizon, casting the two climbers into a long shadow. They didn't have time to go around. They'd freeze to death before they got to the object. "We need to rope up," Cole stated.

"Agreed."

The two checked their harnesses and clipped into their 50ft climbing rope. Cole was glad that he'd grabbed the rope from the downed helicopter. Once assured they were firmly secure to their lifeline, the two set out again, Crocker took the lead.

"So, you were telling me about your dad's time with the 509," Cole reminded.

"Oh, yeah. So, it's the height of the Cold War, America is deeply worried about a Soviet first strike or invasion. My dad's job was to investigate UFO reports to ascertain whether there was a Soviet connection to the lights and craft people were seeing across not just the United States but the entire planet."

"Soviet connection? You think the Soviets are behind the UFO phenomena?"

"No I don't. But in the late eighties the U.S. military did and that's all that matters. In fact, in 1947 the U.S. military was deeply concerned about Soviet driven UFOs. Do you know why?"

"Enlighten me," Cole offered.

"Do you remember Orson Wells?"

"Do you ever stay on topic?" Cole asked.

Crocker wasn't amused, crossing her arms in disgust.

"Yes, I know Orson Wells," Cole admitted. "Director, actor, writer of Citizen Kane. One of my favorite movies."

"Did you know Mr. Wells got his entertainment start in radio, not movies?"

"Sure wasn't he the genius behind the radio drama War of the Worlds?"

"One and the same," Crocker confirmed. "In 1938 Wells produced a radio drama of H. G. Wells' <u>War of the Worlds</u>. However, Mr. Orson Wells in what could be seen as the first reality program downplays the drama aspect of his show, and highlights the reality. Wells' radio program starts with a news flash about lights and a strange craft over New Jersey. It quickly cuts to the scene where an on the ground reporter confirms the landing of an alien craft and the appearance of alien beings. These beings intentions aren't immediately known but they quickly go on a killing spree and the military is called in."

"Go on," Cole urged.

"Now remember this is all fiction. Wells is spinning his fabrication from the RCA radio studio in New York city. There wasn't one shred of truth to the broadcast. Do you know what happened next?"

"Wide spread panic," Cole conceded.

"Give the man a cigar! Yep, wide spread panic. People believed the country was under attack. They made runs on their grocery stores, grabbing anything and everything for the pending attack. They stocked up on ammunition and hunkered down in their basements. UFO sightings and reports of fire fights with alien invaders began to flood local police stations. Except it was all bullshit. The invasion was fake, but the panic and terror it produced in the American public was real."

"If I seem to remember correctly, it made Wells an instant star, capturing the American public's attention," Cole said.

Crocker continued her story undeterred by the building storm. "However almost right after the War of the World's broadcast, World War II broke out in Europe. The United States' attention was focused on defeating the real and present threat of Nazi Germany and Imperial Japan. The fear and panic over invasion was heightened even more."

"Makes sense," Cole concurred.

"During the war, the United States and the allies spent huge time and energy in technology research. The Manhattan Project being the most famous. The United States feared Germany's building of the atomic bomb. However, by the end of the War the United States learned that the German atomic program really never got off the ground. Germany simply couldn't muster the enormous amounts of resources and energy necessary to build the bomb. In the end, World War II Germany wasn't in a position to build a bomb. Yet, Germany did see some amazing military developments. Do you know where?"

"Aviation?"

"Not just aviation although their breakthroughs in jet propulsion and drone technology were amazing, but their most impressive work was in ballistic missiles. The German rocket and aviation scientists developed technology decades ahead of anything the allies had at the time."

She waved her hand mimicking a streaking aircraft. "They built jet fighters capable of approaching the sound barrier. They built rockets that carried explosive payloads to the edge of space, reigning terror down on London and other British cities."

Crocker turned to face Cole, emphasizing her next point. "All these advancements took place over a matter of a couple dozen months. As the war wound down, the allies and the Russians were in a race to be the first to secure Nazi research facilities and scientific laboratories."

Crocker knelt down and drew a map of Germany in the snow. "Berlin is here," she said pointing to a dot roughly midpoint of her snow map. "The Russians overran Berlin in April 1945, and secured many of Germany's most prized scientific secrets and facilities and scientist themselves. Meanwhile, the United States and Great Britain controlled the Western half of Germany and most importantly the missile test sites at Peenemunde." Crocker made another dot on Germany's Baltic Sea Coast. "Peenemunde, as you probably remember, was the site of the Nazi's V2 rocket factories and launch sites."

"Of, course," Cole replied with a slight role of his eyes.

"The Americans and British got their hands on Nazi rocket scientists like Von Braun, the man I told you who put America on the moon, and others. But more importantly they got tantalizing insight into what drove Nazi aviation advancements."

"Let me guess, little green men?" Cole joked.

"Make jokes if you want, but the Americans found facilities at Peenemunde and Mittlewerk that hinted at advanced technologies such as particular accelerators and anti-gravity engines. The most famous being the Nazi Bell. Allied captured Nazi's, under interrogation, reported the Bell was an advanced aircraft or propulsion device. These POW's reported the Germans reversed engineered the Bell from a UFO that crashed in Germany during the 1930s. If that was the case, it would explain why German aircraft and rocket technology exploded during the war."

Crocker stood up and stretched her back. The long climb to the object and the toll of being swept up in an avalanche, falling into a crevasse, and crashing in a helicopter was beginning to tax her strength.

Cole placed a gloved hand over his mouth and rubbed his cheeks in a not so hidden sign of disbelief. "Okay, well what happened to the Nazi Bell?"

"No one knows. Some believe the Nazi's destroyed it before it fell into Russian hands. Others argue the German's moved it to a more secure underground location in the German Alps where it sits today awaiting discovery. Still others say the Nazi's whisked it off to Argentina before the end of the war. Or perhaps the Russians got ahold of it. Or my personal favorite is the United States, like that scene at the end of Raiders of the Lost Ark, has the Bell locked away in some super-secret research facility. Where ever the Bell may be today, there can only be one conclusion; the Germans' rocket program had a little divine intervention." Crocker made air quotes when she stated the word divine.

Crocker stepped over a small crack in the ice. Her forward foot came down and broke through a snow bridge, causing her to lose her balance and stumble.

"Careful!" Cole yelled out expecting Crocker to once again be swallowed up by a crevasse, but Crocker caught her step and stopped her fall. The obvious snow bridge held and she continued on her way.

"Come on," Crocker encouraged with a wave of the hand. The bridge will hold. Cole wasn't so sure, but looking around realized he didn't have much choice.

The storm would be on them shortly and the two of them needed to find shelter and soon.

They cautiously continued on their way.

"Okay, so let's just say, for argument, the Nazi's had "divine" intervention helping their rocket program, but what does that have to do with the object over there?" Cole was still convinced the thing was some type of wayward military hardware. He again made a mental note to contact the local army base when he got back to headquarters. Someone at the DOD would get a serious tongue lashing when this was all said and done.

"So, at the conclusion of the war, the Russians and Americans learned at least one lesson from the Nazi's. They were both woefully behind the curve on rocket development. In the subsequent years after the war, the two countries were locked in a race to be the first into space. The Russians' initially appeared posed to capture the high ground so to speak. They put the first satellite in orbit, the first animal, the first man and the first woman into space. They were also first in achieving manned orbital flight and other milestones like space walks and docking maneuvers."

Cole said nothing.

"By the start of the 1960's, it appeared the Russians would be first to the moon and likely have the ability to build military bases in space from which to rain nuclear weapons down upon any target they chose."

Cole listened intently. He could see Crocker was on a roll.

"But almost as miraculous as the Nazi's development of the rocket technology, by the end of the sixties the United States had not only caught the Russians, they surpassed them, landing 12 astronauts on the moon."

"Well at least you believe the United States actually went to the moon," Cole kidded. "You'd be amazed at how many visitors I've met who believe the whole things was filmed on a Hollywood backlot studio."

"Of course I believe in the moon landings. I'm not crazy," Crocker countered. "Besides, maybe the U.S. could pull off one faked moon landing, but six? No way!"

Cole made a slight nod of agreement. "You got me there."

"Anyway, things just got more intense after the moon landing. Advancements in high speed, high altitude aircraft really took off, no pun intended." Crocker said with a wink of the eye. "The United States appeared to develop some new high performance plane, advanced stealth technology, or unmanned aerial vehicle about every decade."

Cole could see the wheels really turning in Crocker now. Cole half expected smoke to pour from his climbing partner's ears. The ranger guessed that she had been waiting years for an audience to present her grand conspiracy theory.

"Nearly all of these developments took place in a place called Skunkworks at Area 51 in the Nevada National Security site. Advanced aircraft is just part of what was developed at Area 51. A huge part of the government's work at the Security Site centered on nuclear bomb research. Most people don't know this but nuclear detonations on the security site were a nearly monthly occurrence. In fact, nearly 1,000 nuclear blasts have rocked that part of Nevada. It's the most heavily nuked part of the free world. In fact, one section of the security site, Area 11, is so contaminated with radioactive material it is called Plutonium Valley. Cute huh?"

Cole again didn't say anything.

"Other nuclear tests included high altitude detonations, underground blasts, mock attacks on enemy bombers and on and on and on. The bombs just became bigger and bigger and bigger. At one point, nuclear scientists worried that their bomb might ignite the atmosphere and reduce the entire earth to a cinder. They brushed aside the concerns and went forward with the test anyway. Again, advancements came fast and furious, almost like clockwork and all too regular to be another coincidence."

Crocker appeared to come to the end of her speech. Cole's head hurt keeping track of the multiple spinning parts and actors. The FBI, NSA, CIA, Departments of Defense and Energy, NASA, every Presidents since Roosevelt, the Soviets, the Nazi's, Men in Black, advance aircraft, ballistic rockets, the moon landings, UFOs and aliens all connected in an elaborate web of conspiracy and deceit. A secret that Crocker believed would stop the world on its axis. The answer to this conspiracy, the puzzle piece that would bring the picture into focus and blow the lid off 70 years of lies and secrets, lay just down this ridge.

Cole found the entire story incredible. It didn't quite mesh. Cole didn't see the all-encompassing connecting threat, but he knew one thing, Crocker believes she did.

Cole looked up and could see the object more clearly now. It was only a few hundred yards away now. It was glistening in the distance. He had to admit that it didn't appear to be like any military equipment he'd seen before. Not that Cole was an expert on military hardware, but as he'd told Crocker he'd seen his share of park placed radar tracking, communications, and weapons systems. This was different than anything he'd seen before.

It was hard to describe. It was black but with an extremely high reflective appearance. The craft looked flawless, without so much as a scratch on its surface. As Cole climbed closer to it, it appeared to shimmer and shine resembling a mirage, almost as if the craft was somehow impacting the light around it, trying to hide its presence from all prying eyes.

Cole knew enough about quantum physics to understand that light can be bent or manipulated by objects, but usually to bend light it would require an object with extremely high mass, usually something the size of a star or dense like a black hole. This object was only about the size of a two story house. *Odd*, he thought.

As he got closer, Cole noticed the air felt electrically charged, like millions of tiny pin pricks were hitting the exposed skin on his face. It was incredibly painful, but it was apparent the object was not only having an impact upon the light of the surrounding area, but also the electric charge of the atoms within its nearby surroundings. *Really odd.*

The two continued to approach the object. Closer and closer now. Cole noticed a metallic taste building in his mouth. Made sense given the electric charge. "You taste that?" Cole asked Crocker.

"Yes, it's similar to what I experienced the first time I visited the object," she confessed. "Very unsettling but the sensation eventually passes."

"Good to know," Cole responded. He was truly happy to know the taste would subside as it was starting to make him a bit sick to his stomach.

Finally, when they were nearly on top of the object, Cole noticed a low level buzz, like the sound a mechanical purring cat might make. "I assume you hear the buzz as well?" Cole asked.

"Yep, again that's what I experienced the last time I was here," Crocker reassured.

They stopped a few feet from the object. Cole dropped his pack on the ground. He rummaged through what was left of its contents. Not much but a couple granola bars, a canteen and a half of water. A flash light, some matches, a rain poncho, and his 9mm pistol. He looked over the pistol. All appeared to be in working order. Cole doubted he'd need it, but standing at the base of a 20ft tall, jet black pyramid like object made him begin to question whether Crocker's story might be true.

He'd never seen anything like the object before. It sat on the lip of a deep crevasse, cracked open during the recent avalanche. Cole kicked a small rock into the abyss, hoping to hear it hit bottom.

Nothing.

"Watch your step," Cole warned. "Fall in there and one is likely to become a permanent resident on the mountain."

"Will do," Crocker responded.

Cole continued to inspect the outside of the object. It was strange; there was something otherworldly about it. Cole couldn't quite put his finger on it, but then it hit him. The object had no seams, no rivets, no panels. At least nothing that could be detected. It was as if the object was constructed out of single piece of material. That too was odd. The material was unlike anything he'd seen before. It wasn't metal, nor was it plastic. It didn't appear to be carbon fiber either, but that was the closest material he thought it resembled.

Cole took off his glove and felt the object's surface. It was incredibly smooth. He could discern no resistance as he slid his fingertips across it surface. Almost as if his fingers floated just above its exterior. It was also warm to the touch. Warmer than it should be he realized.

"That's weird," Cole muttered.

"What? What is it?" Crocker asked.

Cole continued to slide his hand across the object's surface. "Well, this object is warm. Both the side in

218

the sun and shade feel about the same temperature. Warmer than the surrounding air obviously. Like it has an internal power source."

Crocker felt the object's surface as well.

"But what's really strange," Cole went on looking down at where the object met the snowline "is that it's not melting the snow. Shouldn't the objects higher temperature melt any snow and ice around it? Either my sense of touch is off or this object is defying normal thermal dynamics."

"Your sense of touch isn't wrong," Crocker confirmed. She walked to the back of the object, the side in the shade. "Come here and take a look at this."

Far off in the distance, Cole heard the sound of falling rock. To the untrained ear it might have resembled the sound of a waterfall, but it was most certainly rock fall. Cole scanned downslope to see where the rock fall might be located. It appeared to be coming from around the helicopter wreckage.

The fire was still burning, that was easy enough to make out, but the source of the rock fall wasn't so easy to establish. *Could someone still be alive at the wreckage?* Cole wondered. No that couldn't be it he decided. He personally confirmed that all had been killed in the crash. He was certain of it.

Perhaps, rescuers had reached the crash site faster than anticipated. Cole dispensed with that notion as well. They had heard no helicopter since they left the crash site, and none of his ranger's would have reached it in the time since the helicopter went down. If there was someone up here, they had to have been on the mountain when the crash occurred, but with the storm building, they wouldn't be able to provide much help until it passed. Cole and Crocker would have to survive the immediate future by themselves.

While the idea of sharing another night huddled together with Crocker had its appeal, this time would be even more tenuous as it appeared they'd be out in the open without so much as a sleeping bag.

Cole continued to stare off in the direction of the rock fall. For a brief moment, high up on the ridgeline where he and Crocker had just descended from, Cole saw what appeared to be a mirage. The air on the ridgeline seemed to flicker and warp if just for second, but as quickly as it appeared the specter had disappeared. The ranger wiped his eyes. *It's got to be the altitude, or the stress playing tricks on my eyes,* he thought.

**Mount Rainier Ridgeline, May 5th, 7:15 a.m.**

The Tall Man cursed under his breath. He'd clumsily kicked loose a couple of rocks. Mere pebbles actually, but it had been enough to start a small cascade of debris raining down the ridgeline below him. He stopped dead in his tracks, hoping his prey far below had not heard his error. No luck. The ranger had heard the cascade and turned toward the Tall Man's direction. This ranger's senses were obviously quite good and attuned to his environment. The Tall Man made a mental note to be more careful and not underestimate the ranger. He could be trouble.

The Tall Man watched as the ranger continued to scan and search in his direction. However, the Tall Man's light bending camouflage was obviously working. The ranger couldn't quite make his target out. The Tall Man could see the ranger was aware something wasn't right. He was staring directly at the Tall Man, but it was apparent he couldn't figure out the source of the rock fall.

The Tall Man surmised the ranger would likely chalk it up to the wind. Just to be certain, the Tall Man adjusted the controls on his uniform. His clothes advanced technology bent light, making the person wearing the camouflage appear invisible. The technology wasn't perfect. Wind, atmospheric conditions, moisture, and even movement could

221

distort the illusion of invisibility and produce mirages or optical illusions. To the trained eye, or anyone familiar with the invisibility camouflage, these distortions were telltale giveaways, but to the untrained, most had trouble understanding what they were seeing. Their brains lacked the context within which to place the apparent ghost. Most simply dismissed the mirage as optical illusions or tricks of their mind. The Tall Man could see the ranger was thinking exactly this.

The Tall Man turned his attention to the smoldering helicopter that lay just a few dozen yards behind him. He'd come to the edge of the ridgeline to see how far ahead his prey had gotten. He assured himself they had not gotten too far. He was disappointed to see that they had found the object. With the storm building, they wouldn't be getting off the mountain with this news anytime soon. He had some time.

He walked back to the helicopter, now not much more than a crushed hulk. The three bullets he'd put in the engine section had nearly done what he needed it to. The copter was down, and almost all onboard were dead. However, two had survived. Two loose ends remained. Not to worry, he'd tie those up shortly. In the meantime, he searched what remained of the downed craft. Perhaps there was something of use in the wreckage. Something he could use to finish his job.

The fire consuming the craft had died down considerably. The Tall Man determined that the fuel had ignited and fed the blaze. Once it had been exhausted, the inferno diminished considerably. This allowed the Tall Man to search the cabin and crew compartment in relative safety.

The Tall Man began his search in the cockpit. Most of the helicopters avionics, its navigation and communications equipment was smashed beyond repair. The electrical system including the emergency backups were not working, as none of the gauges registered any readings. The craft for all intents and purposes was dead. The Tall Man pushed the pilot out of the left side door. The woman's semi-charred body fell with a thump, sliding across the wet snow. The Tall Man rummaged around the pilot's former chair. He found a few maps, a pair of sunglasses, a coffee mug, and an Ifly.com ball point pen. He tossed all these on the floor.

The Tall Man climbed over the co-pilot chair to the crew compartment in the back of the helicopter. Two flight nurses were sprawled across the floor. Both were obviously dead. Like the co-pilot, the Tall Man moved these two out of his way with little thought or remorse. As he'd done in the cockpit, the Tall Man ransacked the crew compartment. Medical equipment such as scalpels, forceps, gauze, and a defibrillator littered the cabin floor. Nothing of any real use, he concluded. The Tall Man scanned the compartment's interior. It wasn't much larger than the back of an average sized van. On the far wall, a bench seat that could accommodate three people was dangling by a single bolt restraint. Behind and above the bench seat and on the far wall of the crew compartment were several built in cabinets. One had a white cross, apparently a storage place for more medical supplies. The other cabinet had no apparent markings. He opened the cabinet doors.

Inside were climbing ropes, water bottles, cold weather jackets and snow pants. Underneath these items was a large duffle bag, marked for the Gifford Pinchot National Forest: Avalanche Control Equipment. A clipboard was attached to the bag. The clipboard contained a pad of paper, sealed inside a watertight Ziploc bag. Through the clear vinyl the Tall Man read a hand written note.

> Thanks to Mercy Flight for carrying these supplies up to the Forest Service in the Cascade Mountains.

He zipped open the bag and peered into its central compartment.

Inside he found exactly what he needed.

## Disappointment Cleaver: May 5th, 8:30 a.m.

Cole continued to stare up toward the top of the ridge, but the apparition, if there had ever been one was now gone. It had to be the altitude playing tricks on his vision but he could have sworn he'd seen something above them on the hill where they had just been. He shook his head in a futile attempt to clear out any cobwebs that may be clouding his vision or judgement.

He knew he was tired and that was affecting his abilities. If he was honest, the stress of their current situation was also affecting his faculties. He wasn't entirely sure how they would survive another day on the mountain's side and that problem was commanding more and more of his mental abilities. It was tiring. He shook his head again. He'd have to think of something and quick.

Cole turned his attention back to Crocker and walked behind the object into the shade. The air temperature was much colder in the objects shadow than on its side facing the sun. Cole's and Crocker's breath formed vapor clouds enveloping their heads, resembling some strange space helmet. "What is it?" Cole asked.

"Look here," Crocker commanded pointing at a three foot square section of the object. "What do you see?"

Cole studied the area closely. He stared at the surface which appeared perfectly smooth. The surface was playing tricks with his eyes as he had trouble really focusing on it. "I don't see anything," he finally concluded.

"Exactly!" Crocker confirmed. "There is nothing there. Isn't that amazing?"

"What are you talking about?" Cole asked. He began to get worried that perhaps the altitude or the gravity of their situation was getting to Crocker. She might be losing touch with reality.

"Haven't you noticed anything odd about the surface?" Crocker asked wiping her hand across the object's smooth exterior.

"Where to start?" Cole began.

"No I mean look at it, the object is perfectly smooth. There isn't a seem, rivet, or joint anywhere on its surface. It's as if the object was created out of a single block of material."

"Yeah, you're right," Cole agreed.

"Yet, I know there is a door here on this side of the object."

"How do you know that?" Cole questioned.

"Because I've seen it. I've been to this object before and was able to open a panel."

"Wait, What?" Cole stated a puzzled look on his face.

"Yes, I was up here yesterday," Crocker began still waving her hand across its surface. "Look I'm not sure what you think is going on, but I'm going to level with you."

"Finally," Cole replied with a sarcastic roll of his eyes.

"Can it!" Crocker declared. "This is serious." She pointed at the object. "This is real and there are people in this world who will kill to keep it hidden. I'm not going to let that happen. Help me find the panel."

"Why?"

"I wasn't able to get inside or even get a good look into the object the last time I was here. However, I'm certain if I can get inside, I'll find something to prove this object is not of this earth. We are standing next to something that will change the world and how humanity sees its place in the universe. My father died trying to reveal its secrets to the world. I won't let him have died in vain."

Cole still wasn't convinced the object was of alien origin. It did look futuristic and unlike anything he'd ever seen before. However, he reminded himself that the B2 stealth bomber would have likely been confused for an extraterrestrial aircraft before it was revealed to the world. Yet, he could see on Crocker's face that she was convinced the object was alien. It was apparent she was on a mission to redeem her father and right now it didn't do any good to dissuade her from that task. Besides, if there was a panel leading to an interior part of the object, perhaps the two of them could find shelter, a place to ride out the storm. The thought crossed Cole's mind that maybe, just maybe, they would survive. He threw himself into finding the door.

"Okay," Cole said. How did you find the door the last time?"

"I don't really know, I accidentally stumbled upon it. However, I wasn't able to get inside before I was swept away in the avalanche. Yet, I believe its touch or sound activated." She pondered her response for a moment and added "come to think of it, it could be light activated as well."

"Swell, anything else that could possibly be the trigger? I think we've included everything but temperature, aroma, and humidity."

"Wait, now that I think of it, I believe it was air pressure or taste activated," Crocker giggled.

"Or perhaps it needs a secret password," Cole stated. He backed up a few steps and he spread his arms as he he'd seen parishioners do in church. "Open sesame," he said in his best Lawrence of Arabia accent.

Nothing happened.

At that both broke into laughter. It was quite ridiculous. Two people trapped on the side of a glacier capped mountain, poking and prodding an obsidian object in the hope of gaining entry. To any outside observer, Cole was convinced they looked perhaps like cavemen grappling over how to tame fire. Cavemen however eventually harnessed fire, Cole wasn't so sure he and Crocker would be as successful.

The jokes lightened the mood of their predicament, if only for a moment. The gravity of their situation, the threat of death returned however and Cole and Crocker returned their attention to getting in the object.

"I'm going to search this area of the object, you mind searching that part?" Crocker stated.

"Of course," Cole replied.

The two threw themselves into reviewing every inch of the objects surface, but this closer inspection only solidified for Cole that the surface was perfectly smooth. There didn't appear to be a seam or section break on its entire surface. Not even a scratch, which was strange considering it had obviously been placed or crashed on the side of the mountain. One would expect some damage when putting it in place. Moreover, one would expect some weathering if this device had been on the mountain for as long as Crocker believed it had. There was nothing, absolutely nothing. It might as well have been placed there just ten minutes ago for all the lacking of scarring it had on its surface. The object's appearance reminded Cole of the show room finish found on new cars, but even more flawless. *I bet many a car salesman would love to know the secret behind this finish,* he thought.

Cole could see Crocker was equally intent upon covering every inch of the object. But it was apparent she too was having no more luck in cracking it open than he was.

Cole looked off to the East. The storm was coming on fast. He checked the thermometer attached to his coat zipper. It read 38 degrees. The mercury had dropped 3 degrees in just the past hour. It was going to get cold quickly.

He returned to the object, but was growing convinced they weren't getting in. It was time for plan "B." Cole took off one of his gloves and wiped his face. He was tired and didn't anticipate getting much sleep the next couple days. He went to pull on his glove, but dropped it. Leaning down to pick it up, he placed his bare hand on the object.

A pulse, like a mild jolt of electricity went through his hand and up his arm. Cole pulled back his hand in surprise. Where he'd placed his hand, a back lite image appeared, just above the object's surface.

"Hey! I think I've found something," Cole shouted to Crocker.

Crocker came running over, "What is it?"

"Look," Cole said pointing at the illuminated panel. On it was an image of what to Cole resembled the outline of a chicken's foot or a tree with three branches coming out of its trunk. "What do you think it means?"

"That's got to be the way in!" Crocker exclaimed.

She edged closer to the image. She removed her glove and made a hand signal that resembled the Vulcan salute. She placed her hand on the "chicken foot" outline, making sure to keep her hand within its outline. The image was roughly one size larger than her hand.

At that a click, followed by a low hiss could be heard coming from deep within the object. *Something was happening,* Cole thought.

The hiss was followed by a low hum, then a pop followed by a louder hiss. The section of the objects surface where the image had been cracked, by his touch, creating a square panel. From behind the panel bright light burst forth pouring out from around the panel's edges.

The square panel lifted off the surface about six inches, hesitated, then slide to the left revealing the interior of the object. Cole watched the panel move up and across the object's exterior. It didn't appear to be supported by any physical mechanism. Cole speculated it was some type of magnetic technology. *Pretty impressive*, Cole thought.

Cole and Crocker poked their head into the object. Inside was a mid-sized chamber roughly the size of a large cargo van. The room contained wiring, lights, display panels, and what Cole assumed were several rows of computer servers and processors. There was enough room to hold both Cole and Crocker, but it didn't appear as if the room was meant to hold passengers. Rather, the empty space was likely meant to allow maintenance workers access to the interiors' computers and other equipment.

Cole looked over at Crocker, tilting his head toward the interior. "After you," he offered.

"Thanks," Crocker replied skillfully and swiftly sliding through the access hatch. Cole quickly followed her.

The inside of the object was tighter than it appeared on the outside, but Cole was happy to see that it would provide sufficient shelter for at least the upcoming evening.

The air in the room was humid and had an organic smell to it, something like freshly plowed soil. It felt like the inside of a greenhouse, warm, earthy, and damp. Cole was amazed to see that the room wasn't coated in algae or some other fungal growth. Perhaps the high altitude was retarding microbial growth, but Cole suspected it was something else.

Cole and Crocker took off their spiked crampons and carried them in their hands. The floor was damp and slippery, but the three inch spikes wouldn't provide any additional traction on the metal like floor.

The two looked around the room. There were no chairs or any other visible infrastructure for a pilot or passenger. "It doesn't seem like this object was meant to hold a crew," Crocker said.

"Agreed," Cole concurred. "Strikes me it's more of a drone than a piloted aircraft."

"Or probe," Crocker said through a frown.

"Perhaps," Cole thought. He continued to look around the interior. Much of the equipment appeared to be brand new and built with cutting edge technology. Cole wasn't a technology expert; oh he knew how to operate his computer, digital camera, and several graphic illustration programs. He'd taken a few GIS classes in college and toured the computer servers for the NPS in Washington D.C. but this was different. Obviously it was much smaller, but something was different. He couldn't put his finger on it, but the technology inside this room was unlike anything he'd ever seen before.

"Look at this," Cole said calling Crocker over to the panel he was studying. The screen was a light green, with blue wires, appearing more like veins pulsing across the panel. It's surface was shiny and reflective, seeming almost liquid. "This resembles living tissue, more than mechanical," Cole stated.

"That's what I was thinking," Crocker agreed. "It's like looking at an internal organ. Really weird."

Crocker scanned the entire room as did Cole. Several similar panels to the one they were inspecting adorned the room walls and even floor. The technology, if it was technology, seemed to be an integration of living and synthetic components. "This is really high tech stuff," Crocker finally said.

"Have you ever seen anything like this before?" Cole asked.

"No, this is super advanced. I'd doubt our government has anything even approaching this technology. And if it does, this is deep black budget stuff."

"What do you think it does?"

"Not sure," Crocker stated. Looking around the room she went on, "However, this room seems to be a processing center. Perhaps this is the central or core memory of the object, it's brain if you will."

That struck Cole as probably right. The room had the appearance of a brain. Row upon row of what he assumed were metallic like computer processing servers, organic nodes, and blue wires or were they veins connecting them all. They were covered by a thin greenish membrane that reminded Cole of frog skin. A blue-green hue of pulsing light gave the chamber an alien dance club type feel. If this technology wasn't alive, it was doing a damn good job of imitating life.

Across the top of the room, just below what Cole took for the ceiling or was it the skull were a series of symbols and marks. They were a series of long black swoops, curls, and dashes. They appeared airy and light and to Cole resembled the patterns campfire smoke makes. The ranger assumed they were a message but not in any language he was familiar with. He just hoped it wasn't a warning of deadly radiation or keep out.

"Any idea what that is?" Cole asked pointing to the smoke signals?

"No, again I've never seen anything like this?" Crocker repeated. "It's amazing though, isn't it?"

Cole just nodded.

"Oh, that reminds me," Crocker said pulling a digital camera from her pocket. "I need to document this; our lives may depend on our being able to prove this object exists." She started to snap off picture after picture. Crocker repeated this process for several minutes, until Cole assumed she'd taken more than a hundred images of this single room.

Cole left Crocker to her documentary work and began to examine the room's walls more closely. From the outside, the object was massive, roughly the size of a two story building. But so far they had only found a single room, similar in size of a large van or truck. Cole was convinced there had to be more inside this object than this one tiny room, but if finding access to the next room was as difficult as finding access to this room they may never locate it.

As he plodded around the room, Cole became more convinced this wasn't an aircraft, at least not one meant for passengers or crew. There were no apparent walkways, handholds, anything. It was obvious that humans weren't meant to be walking around this section of the ship. That meant, if it was some type of airship it must be a drone. A remotely controlled vehicle, for what purpose however, Cole had no idea.

He had nearly completed his review of the room, when he caught a glimpse of something behind one of the frog skinned covered servers. He poked his head behind the server for a closer look. To this point, Cole was struck by the fact that everything in this room had appeared organic, as if it had grown like a culture inside it, but behind the server, Cole found something odd.

"Come take a look at this," Cole said to Crocker.

"What is it? What have you found?" she asked.

"This doesn't seem right," Cole said pointing at a black panel on the wall.

Crocker studied the panel as well. It was the size of a sheet of note paper, with a dark black screen, surrounded by an equally dark frame.

"It looks like an apple iPad to me," Crocker said.

"Me too," agreed Cole. "That's why I find it odd. Everything else in this room," Cole waved his hands in the air, "looks as if it's been grown straight out of the floor. This is the first piece of technology that actually looks familiar, like something you'd find in a computer store."

"Yeah, so what?" Crocker asked.

"You said this "craft" crashed here on Rainier about 70 years ago, correct?"

"Yes," Crocker agreed.

"Well this room is filled with technology that by today's standard is still lightyears ahead of the current standard, except for this," Cole explained pointing at the iPad panel. "However, at the end of the second world war, this panel would have been cutting edge, at least for humans."

"I see where you are going," Crocker exclaimed. "You think this panel may have been added to this room by humans."

"Let's be clear," Cole began, "I think this whole craft was created by humans, but this piece of technology looks so out of place, that means it deserves a closer look."

"Okay," Crocker conceded with a shrug of her shoulders, "Let's assume this craft was built by humans what do you think this panel does?"

"I don't know, but let's find out." Before Crocker could react, Cole reached out and touched the panel with his right index finger.

The panel immediately lit up and displayed an icon system that would be easily recognizable to anyone even remotely familiar with a modern smart phone. On the screen were buttons with images that depicted a globe, a radio tower, a heart, a gear, a battery, and a few others that were unrecognizable symbols.

"What do think these panels mean?" Cole asked.

"Well, I assume the globe, radio tower and the others are for bringing up information on the craft's internal operations.

"Agreed," Cole said. "What do you think this one means?" Cole pointed to an icon at the bottom right of the panel which depicted two side by side vertical rectangles.

"I don't know," Crocker offered.

"I think I do," Cole said reaching out and pushing the double rectangle button.

"Wait," Crocker began. Yet, before she could finish her protest a previously hidden door just to the left of the panel slid open revealing another room.

"Door," Cole stated with a slight grin.

"How could you be certain that's what it meant?" Crocker objected.

"I wasn't but it seemed reasonable. Remember I'm still not convinced this craft was constructed by E.T. The icon looked like a door to me, so I pushed it and presto we have a door."

"Cute," Crocker said sarcastically. "Let's just avoid pushing any more buttons in the future shall we?"

"Fair enough," Cole said extending his arm in an invite to Crocker to proceed into the next room. "Again, after you."

Crocker took the cue and ducked into the next room. Cole took one last look around their current location and followed behind his comrade.

**Disappointment Cleaver, May 5<sup>th</sup> 9:30 a.m.**

The Tall Man's trek to the object was just as perilous as the two he pursued. He traversed the crevasse Crocker and the ranger recently crossed. He scrambled over the avalanche debris field and dodged a few large boulders before reaching the object's edge. On approach he retrieved his pistol and held it ready in case Cole or Crocker came into view. However, his hopes of ending this pursuit quickly were dashed when he saw the object's open hatch. Apparently, the two were smarter than he'd guessed. This could be more difficult than he thought.

He approached the open hatch with caution and stealth. He wanted to make certain he didn't spook his prey and be forced to chase them further. This hunt would end here.

A quick glance through the open hatch revealed an empty room. Another open door could be seen in the far wall. "Damn," he hissed, but he assured himself they wouldn't get far before he caught them. Yet, he knew it was only a matter of time before a rescue would be attempted, so the Tall Man decided to set the first part of his plan in motion.

He dropped the duffle bag he'd picked up from the downed helicopter. It landed in the snow with a soft thud. He was happy to drop the load. It had been heavy and difficult getting the bag to the object but it held the tools for tying up the loose end this object had become. He zipped open the bag and revealed its contents. Inside he found a note with Washington Department of Transportation written across the top.

The first paragraph read,

> Enclosed please find 3 High Explosive (HE) M1 105 Howitzer shells for avalanche control at Snoqualmie pass. Please be advised that these shells are different than the normal ordinance used for avalanche control as they have higher explosive potential. Please handle with caution.

"Perfect," he said. "These should do the trick.

The Tall Man pulled one of the shells out of the box. It was a dull green with 105 H in yellow letters stenciled across the bottom. The top of the shell was crowned with a dull black fuse. The shell was lighter than he expected. He guessed it weighed 40 pounds, but it didn't feel like it. Perhaps it was a lighter construction since it was to be used in avalanche control, rather than warfare. No matter, he was certain it would do the trick.

The Tall Man circled the object to the point where it neared the newly created crevasse. He set down the shell and began to dig a hole in the snow between the object and the crack in the ice. After about five minutes of digging he had a hole roughly big enough to hold his body. He placed the shell at the bottom of the hole. He repeated this process with two other shells, placing one at the object's mid-point along the crevasse and the other at the far end.

From his own backpack, the Tall Man retrieved the flashbang grenades he'd salvaged after being swept down the mountain in the avalanche. These were programmable grenades with delayed detonation capabilities. Carefully, removing each of the shells' fuse caps, the Tall Man placed a flash bang grenade into its exposed center. He set the timer for 20 minutes.

That should give him enough time to make certain his prey was dead. If all went according to plan, he'd kill Crocker and the ranger before the shells went off plunging the object into the bottomless crack in the ice to a place where they wouldn't be found for another thousand years.

Double checking the placement of the shells, the Tall Man was convinced they would do the trick. Now he had to make certain his prey, Crocker and the ranger wouldn't escape their fate. He'd debated retreating now, but there was an off chance that the two would evade his plans and return to civilization with proof of the objects existence and its purpose. He couldn't let that happen. He'd have to make certain they were dead and would be buried with the object as well.

He made his way back to the object's doorway. The storm was just now reaching the object. The winds immediately increased, kicking up billowing clouds of blowing ice and snow. Visibility was once again cut to a few feet. No one would be getting on or off this mountain for a while. This was both good and bad news.

The building storm meant his prey wouldn't be going anywhere, nor would they be receiving any more help in the near future.

Yet, on the negative side of the ledger, the Tall Man realized he too would have difficulty getting off the mountain anytime soon.

He gazed into the object's entry way, it looked like a black hole or mouth into the belly of a futuristic beast. He ducked his head through the opening and carefully stepped into the darkened room. He checked his watch as it counted down to the detonation: 19:35, 19:34, 19;33. He'd have to move quickly if he didn't want to end up entombed as well.

## Inside the Object, May 5th, 10:35 a.m.

Crocker and Cole stepped through the door leading into another room. This one was slightly larger than the one they had just left. It was also more recognizable. It struck Cole as something that would be familiar to any person who even moderately follows sci-fi television or movies. There were two seats that seemed about the right size for an average human. In front of the seats, was a control panel, with buttons, knobs, and control sticks. Two pairs of pedals, like those of an airplane could be seen below the control panel.

Cole had spent some time flying when he was younger and the room's set up struck him as similar to the flight deck of a large commercial jet, only far more advanced. Cole entered the obvious cock-pit and sat in the left-hand seat. Crocker grabbed the other. Seatbelts and armrests were attached to the seat. The seats' headrests contained what appeared to be plug-ins for supplemental oxygen and other systems that Cole didn't recognize.

In front of Cole was a dark display screen, similar to the one they had encountered on the object's surface. Cole glanced over to Crocker, she returned the gaze knowing what he planned to do.

"Go ahead," she agreed. "Let's see what happens."

Cole placed his hand on the screen and the monitor immediately came to life. The room was instantly bathed in a pale green light as the object's systems came online. The readings and instruments blinked on and off a few times but eventually the system seemed to gain its footing, as if waking from a long sleep. The panels became fully activated and buzzed like it appreciated its two occupants waking it up.

"Feels a little like we are letting the Genie out of the bottle," Crocker admitted.

"Yeah," Cole had to admit.

He studied the display panel. He recognized several of the gauges and instruments.

"This looks like an altimeter," Cole said pointing at one round image. "While I assume this is the airspeed, rate of climb, and headings indicators."

"Hmm," Crocker uttered.

"As to the rest of the panel, well your guess is as good as mine. But apparently this is the command deck of some type of aircraft."

"That's what I've been telling you all along. However, it's not an aircraft, it's a space ship."

"Perhaps," Cole still wasn't convinced this craft was of extraterrestrial origin, but given what he'd seen in the previous room, the chances this craft was from off planet had obviously increased.

Cole began to poke around the control panel. Touching the airspeed indicator with his index finger, caused the panel to zoom into the gauge. The other gauges shrank and were moved to the left. It was similar to what touching some smart phone apps look like when they fire up. He double touched the airspeed indicator to see what would happen. As on a smart phone, the gauge closed. All the instruments resumed their normal location on the panel.

At the bottom right hand corner of the panel was an icon that looked like a small wheel.

"That looks like the system's icon from my computer," Crocker stated. "Do you think…"

"One way to find out," Cole replied and touched the button.

"Sistemnyy Analiz," a metallic non-gender voice said from speakers in the cockpit ceiling.

Both looked around startled by the robotic voice. It didn't seem to come from a speaker or specific location. Rather the voice emanated from the object itself. As if the object was talking to Cole and Crocker.

"Wait a minute," Crocker said pulling out her iPhone from her pocket. "Push that button again."

Cole pushed the system's icon again. Crocker held her iPhone up to the speaker.

"Sistemnyy Analiz," the voice said again.

"Suri? Please translate," Crocker asked.

"Sistemnyy Analiz," Suri began means "Systems' Analysis in Russian."

"Russian," Cole asked. "You know what this means?"

"Yes, we better get the hell out of here," Crocker said. Both turned toward the exit only to find it blocked by a Tall Man dressed entirely in white, a 9mm pistol held in his right hand.

"No one is going anywhere," the man said.

**Inside the Object, May 5th, 11:00 a.m.**

Cole saw the Tall Man blocking their exit. He was roughly a head taller than Cole, but appeared to be about the same weight. A bit slight for his size, which was a good thing, Cole thought. If he could disarm the man, perhaps he could over power and subdue him, but first he'd have to disarm him.

"The Man in Black, I assume," Cole joked to Crocker.

"In the flesh," Crocker replied. "Believe me now?"

"Shut up!" the Tall Man howled.

"Not very polite, Mr. Man in Black. Nothing like your counterparts in the movies," Cole continued to joke.

"Cute," the Tall Man countered. "Now shut up. Why don't the two of you take a seat on the floor." He paused a moment, smiled and sarcastically said "Please."

"Now that's better," Cole replied. He nodded his head to Crocker urging her to comply with the request. As long as the Tall Man held the gun, it was best for the two of them to do what he wanted. "I'm Ranger Cole. This is Aimee Crocker." Cole pointed to his partner with his thumb. "Although I suspect you already know Ms. Crocker. What should we call you Mr…?"

Cole saw a black military style name plate on the Tall Man's jacket. It was an odd jumble of consonants with no vowels, something like WRFTXVN. It struck Cole as similar to a license plate rather than a name badge.

"That's unimportant," the Tall Man said coldly. "What's more important is what the two of you have discovered about our craft here, and who you might have told. I hope for your sake the answer is nothing and nobody."

At that Crocker stood up, "Fuck off! We know what's going on! We know the Russian's are involved and that this craft represents a threat to national security." Crocker held up her phone and pressed play.

Suri said, "Sistemnyy Analiz."

"Sound familiar, Comrade?" Crocker taunted. "It should because that's Russian for system's analysis." Her forehead furrowed just a bit, "Why would a supposedly alien craft have a computer that speaks Russian, I wonder?"

"Ah, that's disappointing," the Tall Man replied. "Please sit back down."  He jabbed the gun into

Crocker's ribs making her lose her balance and tumble back to the floor.

"I sure hope you haven't told anyone about what you've uncovered," the Tall Man warned.

"Of course, we have!" Crocker bluffed. "I've been documenting everything and live streaming what we've uncovered. "I bet half the world is watching this right now!"

With unbelievable speed the Tall Man snatched the iPhone from Crocker's hand. Crocker didn't even have time to react before the Tall Man was already accessing her phone's apps and files.

"Hey, that's mine! Give it back you fucker!" Crocker yelled while getting to her feet.

Again with cat like reflexes, the Tall Man shoved Crocker back on her butt. "Sit down!" He pointed the pistol directly at her forehead.

The Tall Man's fingers danced across Crocker's iPhone screen. He brought up programs and files. He accessed her email, camera and social media accounts.

"You have taken many troubling pictures and videos, Ms. Crocker, but from what I can see you haven't uploaded or emailed them to anyone. This is good." The Tall Man said through a smile.

"Yeah, well perhaps I sent them through a different email system? Or perhaps I uploaded them on a different phone, smart guy!"

"I doubt it," the Tall Man said rubbing his chin. "I've been watching the two of you for more than a day and you have only used the one phone. Besides, as I'm sure my Ranger friend here will confirm, there is limited cell service up here at 14,000ft. So let's stop the lies and start telling the truth shall we? It will go much easier for the two of you if you do."

"Easier? How do you figure?" Crocker scoffed. "The way I see it, once you get the information you want, we're both dead." Crocker used her thumb to indicate Cole and herself.

"Yes, I'm afraid that's the case," the Tall Man replied his voice calm and without emotion. "It has to be that way."

Cole spoke up at this point, "Why? Why does it have to be that way? And if it is to be the case that Crocker and I are to die up here you owe us the truth about what the hell is going on."

The Tall Man laughed at that. "No I don't. I don't owe you anything. Your logic is flawed and assumes you matter, but there are forces at work here, larger than you can possibly imagine."

The Tall Man dropped Crocker's cellphone and crushed it under his boot.

"You're going to pay for that you asshole!" Crocker yelled.

"Doubtful," the Tall Man replied through a tight smile.

Cole stopped listening to Crocker and the Tall Man's argument over who would pay for the phone. Rather, he thought to himself that he'd heard similar arguments, justifications really from the terrorists he'd brought down trying to ignite the Yellowstone super volcano and those wanting to start America's second Civil War. He'd made a decision that his best plan of action was to keep the Tall Man talking. As long as he was talking, they weren't dead. And the longer they weren't dead, the more time he had to figure out a plan.

"That's okay, I get it," Cole mocked.

"You get what?" the Tall Man answered with an annoyed voice.

"You're not in charge and don't know the purpose of your mission," Cole asserted. "You can drop the pretense that you have any understanding of what's going on here."

The Tall Man laughed again. "You are quite clever, Ranger…?"

"Cole."

"You are quite clever Ranger Cole, but your psychological jujitsu won't work on me. I couldn't care less what you think about me, my mission, or my position in the organization."

"So there's an organization, behind your efforts. Thank God! I was beginning to think we were dealing with a lone nut. Glad to know there are others who can hold you accountable for your delusions," Cole goaded.

"Cute," the Tall Man replied with a sigh. "Again, you're fishing in empty waters Ranger Cole. However, my patience is just about finished and I'm growing annoyed with our conversation."

"Annoyed? Interesting that's something I wouldn't think you possessed."

The Tall Man said nothing, so Cole filled the silence.

"Annoyance is a basic "human" emotion," Cole continued stressing the word human. "Something you seem incapable of being in our short time together."

Just for a second Cole thought he'd seen a flash of anger register in the Tall Man's eyes. However, just as quickly as the fury had risen, the Tall Man regained his composure and the rage was gone.

"Very good Ranger Cole, you are managing to get under my skin. Because of that I'm sorry to inform you our conversation, however entertaining, must come to an end," the Tall Man warned.

Cole was glad to hear he'd irritated his opponent. That meant the Tall Man couldn't anticipate every situation and could be thrown off balance. That gave Cole a slim chance that he and Crocker would come out of this alive.

"So soon, just when it was beginning to get interesting," Cole stated. He began to unclip the water bottle from his belt. "Do you mind if I have a drink? I hate getting shot when I'm thirsty."

Cole didn't wait for a response. He removed the stainless steel Sierra Club water bottle from his belt. When full the bottled weighed about as much as a couple of softballs. *It wasn't much but it would have to do,* Cole thought.

"Do you mind if I stand up? My legs are beginning to cramp," Cole lied.

Again, the ranger didn't wait for the Tall Man's answer. Rather he stood straight up while removing the lid from his water bottle. He brought the bottle up to his lips. Yet, he didn't drink. In a flash, he cocked his arm back and threw the bottle with as much force as he could muster at the Tall Man's head.

The bottle tumbled violently through the air, spewing a fountain of water as it twisted and turned. Instinctively, the Tall Man raised his right arm and hand to block the bottle. It struck his forearm and bounced harmless away. Before he could recover his composure, Cole sprang and threw his entire weight upon the man. Both tumbled to the ground.

Cole scrambled to gain an advantage over his opponent. Cole grabbed the Tall Man's right wrist, the one holding the gun and tried to wrest the weapon from his grip, but the Tall Man was strong, stronger than Cole anticipated. The Tall Man was big in height, but didn't have what he expected to be an appropriate weight. Cole estimated the man would make a great basketball player, except for being fairly underweight.

What the Tall Man lacked in pounds, he made up for in strength. He easily escaped Cole's grip, shoving the ranger off and onto his back. Cole quickly rolled over bringing himself onto his hands and knees. Before the Tall Man could regain his feet, Cole launched himself again at his opponent, executing a perfect form tackle and pinning the Tall Man again to the floor.

Cole began pummeling the Tall Man with punches about the head and gut, but to no effect. The Tall Man absorbed every blow, appearing bored by the assault. The Tall Man finally had had enough and once again threw Cole from on top of him.

The ranger landed in a heap on the floor in a loud thud. Cole had the wind knocked out of him, maybe even broke a rib in the landing. He struggled this time to get to his feet. He prepared himself for the Tall Man's counter assault, but it didn't come.

Cole looked up to see the Tall Man staggering. Protruding from the left side of his skull was a single pair of crampons, the spikes buried in his head to their sole. A red or was it purple liquid oozed from the 10 pencil sized wounds in the Tall Man's head.

Standing next to the Tall Man with a huge grin on her face was Crocker, preparing to bury the remaining crampon into the Tall Man's chest, but before she could inflict another grievous wound, the Tall Man fired his pistol hitting Crocker squarely in the chest.

Cole watched as Crocker fell back, as if in slow motion. A fountain of scarlet blood erupted from her chest and she hit the deck like a bag of wet clothes. Meanwhile, the Tall Man similarly wounded staggered backward a few steps, as if trying to escape from the craft. He only managed a few steps and fell in the adjacent chamber.

Cole rushed to Crocker's aid. She was unconscious, sprawled across the floor on her back. Blood continued to spurt from the hole in her chest. The wound was bad, real bad. Cole pulled off his hat and held it over the wound, but he knew it was hopeless. Crocker had lost too much blood, and unless she got immediate medical attention, the kind one finds in an urban ER, she wouldn't make it through the night.

Crocker took a labored breath, coughed up blood. Cole could tell he was losing her. "Hold on Aimee," he pleaded, but there was little he could do other than beg. She took one more breath, then fell silent. She was gone.

Cole sat dazed, he'd seen death before but this one hit close to home. He'd only known Crocker for a short period of time but he'd grown to respect her drive and tenacity. Her death was a waste.

A rustling sound like someone crawling across the floor could be heard coming from the other chamber. In his effort to save Crocker, Cole had forgotten about the Tall Man. He got to his feet and dashed to the other room.

On the floor, feebly dragging himself toward the exit was the Tall Man. His head and half his body were bathed in the reddish/blue goo, the crampon still buried in his head. An indigo trail of what Cole suspected was blood was created as the Tall Man crawled toward the exit.

Cole could see he'd dropped his gun. Cole picked it up, placed himself between the Tall Man and the exit and pointed the gun at his wounded man's head. "Stop!" Cole ordered.

"You are an annoying man," the Tall Man whizzed. "Get out of my way."

"No, not until I have some answers."

"I told you, you don't deserve answers." The Tall Man continued to crawl toward the door.

"Fine, but Crocker deserves them," Cole growled. "Now fucking stop moving!"

The Tall Man stopped his forward crawl, and rolled over on his back. He leaned against a wall and struggled to lift his head, the crampon still firmly buried in his skull, the blue goo seeping from his wounds now coated nearly his entire skull and much of the right side of his body.

Cole wasn't sure what the liquid actually was, but he was certain it wasn't good for the Tall Man whatever it might be.

The Tall Man reached into his pocket.

"Leave your hands where I can see them ," Cole
barked.

"Or what? You'll shoot me? I'm already dead."

The Tall Man continued to rummage through his
pocket, Cole kept his pistol pointed squarely at the
Tall Man's skull. "I'm warning you!"

The Tall Man looked at Cole with disdain, but kept
digging through his pocket. He obviously found what
he was looking for, pulling out what appeared to be
an iPhone, although it was a model Cole had never
seen before.

The iPhone screen was black and had a slight crack.

"It appears your phone was damaged in our fight,"
Cole chided. "Sorry you won't be able to call
anyone."

The Tall Man continued to ignore Cole and swiped
the screen with his index finger like phone users do to
wake up their machines. His bloody index finger left
a long blue smear across the screen. Nothing
happened.

The Tall Man swiped the screen again, this time with
a bit more force. Again nothing happened. He shook
the device and tried again with the same result. He
pulled the back off the phone and checked the

batteries, which were in the proper place. Jiggling the batteries did nothing to wake up the phone.

"It's not working!" he stated in frustration.

"Problem with your phone?" Cole asked. "It looks like it's just me and you and if you hope to get off this mountain alive, you are going to start talking."

The Tall Man said nothing, but Cole could see wheels were turning in the Tall Man's head. He was apparently thinking about his next step, and his broken phone was hindering his plans.

"Look I'm sure we can work something out, just tell me what the hell is going on here," Cole began.

"You still don't get it do you?" the Tall Man wheezed. "This is much bigger than you or me and I doubt you'd be able to appreciate the significance."

"Fine, then I leave you here and return with the authorities." Cole began to turn and leave.

"No wait!" the Tall Man pleaded. He coughed up more blue goo and spit it onto the floor. "You can't do that."

"I sure the hell can and will."

"No you can't."

"And why not! Give me one good reason!" Cole demanded.

"Humanity's future may depend on you keeping this craft secret," the Tall Man stated.

"Look I've had just about enough with conspiracies, aliens, UFO's and other bullshit! Tell me what the hell is going on or I'm out of here."

Cole again could see the Tall Man considering his situation. He was weighing his predicament and deciding whether he had a choice. "Okay, I've still got a chance to fulfill my mission but it's obvious I won't be able to do that now without your help."

"I'm listening."

"You will probably want to sit down, it's a fairly long story."

Cole was skeptical, "Why don't you give me the reader's digest version."

"Fine, you need to destroy this craft. It's existence can't get out."

"Because it's a Russian craft right?"

"No," the Tall Man coughed out. Cole could see he didn't have much time to live.

"But I heard the Russian announcement."

"So, what?" the Tall Man challenged

"Is the craft American?"

"Nope," the Tall Man answered.

"Well if it's not Russian or American, whose craft is it?"

"It's neither, it's both."

"What, I don't understand," Cole was puzzled. "How can that be?"

"Here's where the story will take some time," the Tall Man began. "You will want to sit down."

Cole continued to stand, but with a flip of his head urged the Tall Man to start at the beginning.

"The story begins at the close of the Second World War, the United States quickly realized it wouldn't always have a nuclear monopoly. The Americans expected the Russians and others to quickly develop their own bombs. Given past history, American leaders at that time believed it wouldn't be long before the world faced another world war, and this time it would likely be the last."

"Everyone knows this," Cole countered.

"What people don't know are the lengths the United States," the Tall Man paused choking and gasping before going on. "The lengths the United States and Russia went to prevent this outcome. The secret partnership they formed to prevent nuclear World War III."

"Partnership? You could have fooled me what with the Korean and Vietnam wars, the Russian invasion of Afghanistan as well as, the Cuban Missile crisis and the Cold War. If that's a partnership, I'd hate to see open aggression."

"The world didn't see open aggression between the two, and that's the whole point of the secret partnership. It's designed to prevent a nuclear war, not all war."

"I don't follow," Cole stated.

"Let's go back farther in time," the Tall Man said wiping the blue blood from his mouth. "What do you know of Operation Paper Clip?"

"Crocker mentioned that," Cole stated glancing over to his dead partner. "Don't tell me the Nazis are part of this secret partnership? The conspiracy gets bigger and bigger."

"Shut up and listen, the fate of the world may hinge on your understanding what I'm about to tell you and your grasping the gravity of our situation."

"I grasp the gravity of our situation just fine, I clearly understand that you killed Crocker and likely several others because you believe your mission is critically important to the world's survival. The only reason I'm even entertaining your wild fantasies is I hope they will explain what the hell is going on here. But don't kid yourself into believing that I buy these Illuminati, Masonic Temple, Trilateral commission conspiracy you're spinning here."

"Actually, those groups are involved as well but only tangentially," the Tall Man stated.

"You're absolutely nuts, you know that?"

"Whether I'm nuts or not doesn't matter, what matters is what you do next. Do you understand?"

"Fine, keep talking."

"So as the Second World War wound down in early 1945, the United States' Army liberated several sites in Western Europe including the Nazi's super-secret rocket test site at Peenemude, Mittlewerks, and the German's heavy water production facilities in Norway. A search of these facilities showed that the Nazis were well on their way toward developing advanced rockets and nuclear weapons. If luck had gone the other way for the Nazis, say they were successful in destroying the British air force during the Battle of Britan, a nuclear Nazi Germany with the ability to hit Russia and the United States would likely have emerged."

Cole considering saying something, but thought better of it.

"The world breathed a sigh of relief at the defeat of Germany and Japan, but leaders in Washington and Moscow knew it was only a matter of time until another war erupted."

The Tall Man shifted his position, closed his eyes and appeared to fall off to sleep. Cole thought he might even be dead, but he reopened his eyes and continued on as if nothing was amiss.

"In 1947, things started to get critical with the Soviet's detonation of their own Atomic bomb. The world was actually on the brink of annihilation. A few leaders high up in the Truman Administration and the Stalin government had learned the primary lesson of World War II; people come together when threatened with an existential threat."

"How do you figure?" Cole questioned.

"Did you know mental health issues in America went down during World War Two or that the Soviets absorbed more than 20 million casualties during the war? The question is why? What connects these two and other countless events? It's that both the United

States and the Soviet Union confronted an external enemy, one that gave their people a common purpose, a central organizing force that allowed them to put aside differences and work for a common goal."

"Makes sense," Cole agreed.

"However, world leaders after the detonations of the Soviet and the Chinese bombs. realized there was no unifying force that could prevent annihilation. Put another way, no terrestrial force could prevent humanities destruction. Some greater threat to all of humanity would be needed to prevent World War III."

"Aliens?" Cole scoffed. "This whole thing is about an alien invasion? You're kidding right?"

"Who said anything about aliens? I said this was about the need for a greater threat."

"I don't follow, and you're beginning to try my patience. You plan on getting to a point anytime soon?" Cole said.

The Tall Man ignored Cole and went on. "Did Crocker tell you about the effect of the <u>War of the Worlds</u> broadcast?"

"Yes, the broadcast caused a wide spread panic."

The Tall Man stared blankly at the ceiling, "I got to hand it to Crocker, she had a lot of the puzzle pieces and was slowly putting them in place. I assume you've also heard of the Wizard of Oz."

"I've seen the movie."

"And what gave the Wizard of Oz his power?"

Cole thought for a moment and said, "People's belief that he was the great and powerful OZ."

"That's right. The wizard had no real power he was nothing more than an illusion, a magic trick if you will. However, an entire society was built around the assumption that he was powerful. It checked people's behaviors and kept society humming along."

The Tall Man paused at this moment, Cole could sense he was about to learn the true story behind the craft he was now sitting in, he would get to pull back the curtain so to speak and see who or what was pulling the levers of this tale.

"In 1946, President Truman signed the Atomic Energy Act with the purpose being to control the spread of nuclear technology and insure the peaceful application of nuclear power. The act also established the Atomic Energy Commission which assumed from the Manhattan Project the responsibility of managing America's utilization of nuclear energy. The Atomic

268

Energy Commission was also responsible for research on the military applications of nuclear reactions. It set up top secret programs in Nevada that included crashing airplanes containing nuclear bombs to see how radiation would be dispersed."

Cole continued to listen.

"Along with the Atomic Energy Commission, the Air Force and CIA worked on new and advanced aircraft. They stole the Nazi's ideas and designs and improved upon them. These scientists created technology such as the stealth fighters and advanced radar systems, technology that had never been seen before on the planet. However, there are technologies, craft, and other weapons being developed by the Energy Commission that, how best to say this, would appear extra-terrestrial to the average person."

The Tall Man leaned slightly to the right. Cole thought he might lose his balance, but he didn't. "Do you have any water?" the Tall Man whizzed.

Cole handed him a water bottle. The Tall Man drank it down with vigor, like a man who had been lost in the desert for weeks. He went on with his monologue.

"Deep inside the Atomic Energy Commission, which is now the Department of Energy, are several black operations. Programs that are on a "Need to Know" basis. One of these programs produced the craft you are now sitting inside."

Cole looked around the interior of the craft and pondered what the Tall Man was telling. It was conceivable this craft was part of a super-secret government program. In fact, that reality seemed most possible and palatable to the ranger.

"That is why you need to destroy it." the Tall Man coughed out.

"Why?" Again, Cole looked around its interior. "I don't understand why it's necessary to destroy the craft. If it's vital to national security shouldn't it be saved and turned back to the military?"

"Who said this was a military operation? You assume too much, Ranger Cole. No, I can assure you this craft needs to be destroyed before the military gets its hands on it. No one except a handful of, shall we say people in my program, even know of its existence and it must be kept that way."

"Wait," Cole objected. "Surely the Department of Defense and the CIA must know it exists."

"Nope."

"What about Congressional leaders?"

The Tall Man shook his head.

Cole paused for a second, the implications of these revelations were starting to sink in, and he posed the obvious question. "The President?"

"The President isn't on the "Need to Know" list," the Tall Man stated.

"What? How can the president be cut out of the loop?" Cole questioned.

"It isn't the first time the commander-in-chief was barred operational knowledge of a secret program. President Roosevelt was cut out of the "Need to Know" chain for intercepted Japanese communications. President Clinton was rebuffed in his efforts to uncovered information on Area 51. Besides, for this one to succeed, it's critical the President not know of its existence."

"That doesn't make any sense," Cole needled "The president is charged with protecting national security, surely he needs to be aware of any national security program."

"Look I'm going to cut to the chase," the Tall Man began.

"Finally," Cole was exasperated and glad to know he was going to hear the punch line.

"The Atomic Energy Act contains language authorizing the president to create partnerships and alliances for sharing the benefits of nuclear energy with the world. President Truman read these provisions quite liberally and began a black ops program designed to simulate an alien invasion."

"You've got to be kidding? How would the U.S. keep such a program secret? Heck, the American's couldn't keep the Manhattan Project hidden from the Soviets. How do you expect me to believe the Soviets wouldn't blow the lid off this doozey?"

"Because the Soviets were and the Russians now are part of the charade."

Cole was stunned, the Tall Man paused to let the implications of the exposure sink in, then went on, "Like Truman, Stalin came out of World War II shocked by what total war had unleashed on Europe and Asia, but they both knew it was nothing compared to what nuclear war would produce. Both men realized future events could quickly spiral out of control and obliterate humanity, unless," The Tall Man coughed, spitting up more blue goo. He took a drink of water and continued. "Unless future world leaders could be brought back from the brink by an outside, alien threat, one with the power to wipe humanity from the face of the earth. Truman and Stalin decided to keep the program from future presidents and premiers in order to maintain its effectiveness. The more people who know about it, the greater the risk the lid being blown off. Further, any invasion would create insurmountable pressure upon world leaders to unify, if they actually believed the threat was real and eminent."

The Tall Man wiped his brow, his breath became more struggled.

"When nuclear war becomes imminent, when the world appears on the brink of annihilation, it's the job of my covert operatives to convince the world that they are under attack and avert the pending nuclear war."

"So that's what this craft represents? A giant false flag, psych operation, designed to convince world leaders that an alien invasion is imminent so that they won't unleash nuclear Armageddon?"

"Yes, that's basically it," the Tall Man said. "Is it really so hard to believe? There is no cavalry that is going to ride in at the last minute to save us from destroying ourselves. We will have to be the architects of our own salvation."

The Tall Man took a deep breath, Cole thought it might be his last, but despite his labored respiration, he went on.

"So, you are now among the Need to Know and I hope you understand why we need you to destroy this craft. The future of humanity literally depends on it."

Cole continued to process what he'd been told. Could it be true that everything was a giant ruse? That this man across from him, was actually telling the truth ? World peace may depend upon what he does next? But what about Crocker? That wasn't a ruse? She was clearly dead and he couldn't just turn a blind eye to that reality.

"What does Crocker and her father have to do with all of this?" Cole asked.

"Captain Crocker, as you probably guessed, worked for us. However, he wasn't privy to all the program's secrets, most notably it being a false flag operation. His job was to investigate UFO reports, discredit them and the people making the reports. We had to maintain tight control over information about UFOs and this program. Crocker had stumbled upon aspects of the program, most notably that it was a false flag operation partially run by the Russians. We feared he'd concluded that the Russian run UFO operation was a threat to national security and was looking for evidence of this craft, which would blow the operation wide open. What Captain Crocker failed to realize is that it was a joint operation between the two nations. Ms. Crocker seems to have taken up where her father left off, much with the same goal of exposing the truth. We obviously couldn't let that happen."

"So you killed the both of them," Cole hissed.

"That's the pessimistic way of looking at it, I prefer to view their deaths as necessary to protect millions of innocents who could be annihilated in nuclear war."

"Well I bet the Crockers would disagree with your assessment of the necessity of their murder," Cole challenged.

"In the end it doesn't really matter whether they would agree with what's been done, what matters is what will you do now that you understand what's truly going on here," the Tall Man responded.

Cole got up. The Tall Man didn't object. Cole could see the man's situation was deteriorating. "You should let me take a look at that wound." Cole suggested.

The Tall Man waved him away. "I'm fine," he whispered. "Look you don't have much time. I'm sure authorities will be here as soon as this storm lifts. You need to destroy this craft before they arrive."

Cole looked around the craft's interior. He determined the Tall Man wasn't going anywhere and sadly neither was Crocker. "Look I haven't decided what I'm going to do, but I'm going to take a look around the outside of the craft." Cole pulled on his gloves and prepared to head outside. "You said you placed charges around the edge of the craft?"

The Tall Man nodded.

"Alright, I have to check out the situation before I make any decision." Cole got up, convinced the Tall Man was in no condition to go anywhere. In fact, it wouldn't surprise him if the man was dead when he returned.

Cole exited the craft the same way he entered. The outer hatch remained open and Cole stepped out on the snowfield. A full force blizzard had engulfed the mountain. Cole lifted his hand to shield his eyes from the blowing snow and ice. He struggled to see and make his way around the craft.

Slowly he made his way around the back of the craft to where it rested near the lip of the gapping and apparently bottomless crevasse. Cole peered into the abyss and could see several buried explosives. He assumed the Tall Man had placed the ordinance. As expected they were avalanche control shells. Cole had significant experience using these shells. The ranger was convinced the buried munitions would surely obliterate any evidence of the craft. The question was, if he was going to detonate them, how would he do it?

How would he set them off without destroying himself?

Meanwhile, back inside the craft. The Tall Man remained seated. He closed his eyes as if entering into a trance. With his right hand, he grabbed the crampon, which remained nailed to his head. He slowly removed the three inch spikes from his skull. No visible sign of discomfort registered on his face. He uttered no sound of protest as he removed the spikes.

He pulled them free and tossed it on the floor next to him. Ten horrifying holes remained where the spikes had once been. The neon blue goo continued to ooze out of the wounds. On his left wrist, the Tall Man touched what appeared to be a high tech wrist watch. Immediately, his body became bathed in a glowing red light. The light focused on the wounds in his skull. In a matter of seconds the red light shrank the holes, until they disappeared.

Healed, the Tall Man got up and walked over to where he'd thrown his cell phone. He picked it up and proceeded to tap on its small screen. He ran a diagnostic and other repair programs in an effort to repair the connection with the avalanche shells that ringed the craft.

"If Cole won't destroy the craft, I'll insure it's never found by anyone," the Tall Man muttered to himself.

The Tall Man tapped a few more buttons on his phone screen. A red bar indicating a failed connection with the explosives turned to green and blinked connected. The Tall Man smiled at this and headed toward the far wall, in the opposite direction of the door Cole had used to exit the craft. He touched the wall in a non-descript spot, illuminating a panel similar to what Cole and Crocker used to open the hatch. The Tall Man placed his hand on the panel, a door immediately appeared, and he exited through it. He checked his surroundings to make certain Cole didn't see his escape and headed onto the snowfield and away from the craft.

At that moment, Cole was returning to the hatch through which he'd exited the craft. He reviewed the situation of the artillery shells and without a remote detonator; he wasn't sure how to set them off, at least without killing himself in the process. Perhaps that's what the Tall Man wants if in fact, that's likely what he wants Cole thought. But he wasn't going to oblige that wish.

He came around the corner of the craft and spied the hatch. It remained open. He approached and prepared to enter. Just then, the ground began to shake under his feet and Cole was knocked from his feet. He heard three distinct blasts coming from the other side of the craft. "Shit!" Cole muttered, realizing the Tall Man must have set off the shells.

Cole scrambled to his feet, just as the blast of the final shell struck him head on. The ranger was once again tossed off balance. The shell's concussion wave tossed Cole like a piece of paper more than a dozen yards, and smashed him against a wall of solid ice. Cole groaned, the wind knocked out of him from the collision. He was able to lift his head just enough to see the craft begin to move. The crack the craft had been balanced upon opened up and a deep thunder like rumble could be heard coming from deep within the glacier. The ice ledge the craft was situated upon was breaking up. Cole could see it was only a matter of seconds until it was swallowed by the glacier's growing crevasse.

The craft's tilt continued to grow, but as if in slow motion. Like a domino falling over in a vat of honey, the craft made its fateful dive into the abyss. Cole watched as the craft fell into the crack and disappeared from view. The object was followed by a cascade of tons of snow and ice. Cole lay motionless upon the ice, waiting to hear and feel the craft hit the bottom of the fissure. He never did. The hole was hundreds of feet deep and the craft was firmly planted at its bottom.

Snow, ice and rock continued to pour into the fissure, forming a river of material which continued for several minutes until the crack was completely filled, forever burying the craft, Cole assumed both the Tall

Man and Crocker were buried in an ice tomb hundreds of feet thick. No one would be digging them out for centuries, if ever.

As quickly as the ice cascade had begun, it ended. Cole became immediately aware that, along with the snow and ice cascade coming to an end, the storm seemed to have dissipated as well. The gale that just a minute ago threaten to blow him from the mountain, had at least temporarily died down.

*Could the object be affecting the weather as well?* he wondered. He couldn't see how, realizing it was now buried under hundreds of feet of snow and ice. However, given what he'd witnessed the past few days, how could he know for sure.

Yet, for now, other than a slight breeze, what moments ago had sounded like a war zone, now resembled a library. Cole thanked his good luck and lay on the ice for a few moments, catching his breath and taking in the situation. A stream of blood started to trickle down the right side of his face. Cole wiped it off with his glove. He patted his head just behind his ear.

"Ouch!"

He pulled his hand back and examined his palm. It was coated in blood. Cole had hit his head in the blast and it now hurt. Bad. The snow around him was drenched in crimson. The ranger was losing blood and lots of it.

Cole felt dizzy; the world around him began to spin. The loss of blood and the altitude made it difficult for him to keep his eyes open. The eye lids felt extremely heavy. He closed them and drifted off into the darkness.

## Harborview Hospital Seattle afternoon, May 8th, 8:45 a.m.

"Ranger Cole?" a distant voice asked. "Ranger Cole can you hear me?"

Cole's head was pounding and all was encased in darkness. He could slowly feel himself becoming more aware of his body, as if he'd been pulled from his physical form and was only now returning to it. He began to open his eyes, but was startled to be blinded by a painful white light. Cole snapped his eyes shut again.

"Ranger Cole?" the voice repeated, "Can you hear me?"

"Yes I can hear you," he muttered. His voice sounding equally distant.

"That's good, can you try and open your eyes again?"

Cole did as he was told and slowly opened his eyes. He was forced to blink trying to grow accustomed to the bright lights of his room.

Slowly his vision improved and Cole could see a Tall Man in a white lab coat standing over him. He had a pen light in his right hand and was flashing it on and off into Cole's eyes.

—

"Excellent, Ranger Cole. Do you know where you are?"

Cole began to answer but stopped. He didn't know where he was. He tried to sit up but couldn't. His body betrayed his commands and he lay confined on his back.

"Please don't try to move Ranger Cole, you've been through quite an ordeal. Again, can you tell me where you are?"

"No, I'm afraid I don't know where I am," Cole replied. He looked around the room and saw monitors, tubes and hoses, bright lights, a table, couch and chair. He could also hear the beeping and whirling of what he assumed were medical devices. A T.V. with headline news was on in the corner. "Although, from the looks of it, it appears I'm in a hospital."

"Correct, very good," the man confirmed. "You are currently in Harborview General Hospital's Intensive Care Unit. Do you know why you are here?"

"Can't say that I can. Nor can I recall how I got here, or…" Cole trailed off for a moment. "Or where I've been for the past couple days."

"Not surprising. You had quite a bump on the head when you were brought in three days ago. You'd also lost a fair amount of blood. You're lucky to be alive."

"I'll take your word for it," Cole stated. Although the ranger seemed to get the impression that the good Doctor might be disappointed by his progress. "Wait, did you say I've been here for three days?" Cole again tried to sit up, a beeping monitor increased its pitch and frequency.

"Ranger Cole, please relax. You are going to pull out your I.V." The Tall Man put a reassuring hand on Cole's shoulder and gently but firmly pushed the Ranger back onto his hospital bed. He went on, "Yes, you've been here the past several days. The Air National Guard brought you in by helicopter after you were rescued from the slopes of Mount Rainier. Do you remember any of that?"

"No," Cole confirmed.

"What is the last thing you remember?" the doctor pressed.

Again, Cole couldn't shake the feeling that the doctor was after something more, but he chalked it up to the bump on his head and went on. "Well, I remember I was planning a long weekend. I'd checked in at the ranger station to get my climbing permit and it all becomes fuzzy after that. As I said before, I don't remember how I got here."

"Hmm," the doctor muttered.

"Hmm, what?" Cole repeated. His anger and frustration starting to build.

"Well, to be quite frank with you Ranger Cole your loss of memory is a little troubling. I suspect that you may have some permanent memory loss. I'd like to do a few more tests and order an MRI to make sure this is the case."

Cole again thought this statement odd. Shouldn't the doctor order tests to determine if the memory loss could be restored?

"Look, Doc?" Cole began looking at the physicians name plate. "That's weird."

"What?" the doctor asked.

"I can't seem to read your name badge. My head must really be messed up but I can't make out any vowels in your name."

"Okay," the doctor began with some alarm. "So, I assume you don't remember me either?"

Cole felt the doctor's question had some double meaning to it, but he couldn't quite put his finger on it. "No, I've never seen you before."

The doctor raised one eyebrow, "I'm not absolutely sure about this memory loss, Ranger Cole. I'm afraid we are going to need to do a full brain scan. I'm going to change your I.V., so we can get you sedated for the procedure."

"Doc," Cole protested. "I just woke up from what you tell me was a three day nap. If it's all the same to you, I'm not all that excited about going back to sleep. I'd like a second opinion."

The doctor ignored Cole's objections, "I'm going to get the meds for the I.V. drip. I'll be right back."

The doctor spun on his heels and strode out of the room. Cole watched him go, thankful to see the back of the doctor. Something wasn't quite right about the man, and Cole would be damned if he'd let the hospital put him back to sleep. Heck he'd just woken up and needed to get clarity on a few things before he consented to anything.

Cole's attention was pulled to the news caster on the TV in the corner. The middle aged African American woman was talking about a crisis between the United States and Russia. Cole figured the trouble, which he had no memory of, had passed and that military tensions were winding down. The anchor cut to another story, Cole grabbed the T.V. remote and turned up the volume.

> "In other news," the woman began, "the world's attention has been captured by reports of UFOs appearing over several international capitols. American officials say there is nothing to be concerned about and the strange lights are related to recent solar flares."

The door to Ranger Cole's room opened again. This time a young female doctor walked in. Cole turned down the TV.

"Look Doc," Cole began before the woman even got halfway across the room. "I'm not sure about the brain scan. I just woke up and would like to get my bearings before we run any invasive tests."

The female doctor had a perplexed look on her face, as if she just seen something disturbing. "What are you talking about Ranger Cole?"

"The other doctor said he was ordering a brain scan and going to get me sedated for the procedure," Cole explained.

"What other doctor?"

"The tall one, pale skin, scars on the forehead," Cole described.

"We don't have anyone like that tending your care. I would know since I'm the lead on your case," the young doctor assured. "Ranger Cole you've suffered a moderate concussion, and from what you telling me, I'm concerned you may be hallucinating."

"Come on, Doc. He was just here. He exited the room, just before you walked in. Surely you saw him in the hall?"

"Mr. Cole, I was at a work station just down the hall. We have this room under closed circuit surveillance. There's been no one in here but myself and your nurses for the past three days. I can assure you of that." The doctor busied herself with some charts, making notes and flipping pages.

Had he imagined the entire interaction with the other doctor? Cole wondered. *Weird.*

"Hey Doc?" Cole asked.

The doctor stopped what she was doing and looked at her patient, "yes?"

"How long before you estimate I'll make a full recovery?"

"Well, given you've had a pretty significant blow to the head, I'd say a week or two. However, I'm concerned your memory loss of the past several days may be permanent."

"Okay," Cole said with a slight nod of the head.

"Why?" the doctor asked.

"Well the way I look at it, I missed out on my long weekend. I'm thinking about going on a climb. Maybe up to Camp Muir."

## Mittlewerk Rocket Production Facility, Nazi Germany April 16, 1945

The U.S. Third Armored Division and the 104th Infantry Division pulled into Nordahusen Germany earlier in the week. Nordahusen was the location of the Mittlewerk Rocket Production facility and the location where Nazi Germany built the dreaded V1 flying bomb V2 ballistic missiles at the closing months of the war.

As they entered the production facility, the tank column and infantry spread out like water on a table. The GI's like ants swarmed over the facility's building, hangers, production areas, and storage sheds. Anything that had walls and ceilings they searched. Throughout their exploration of the town they discovered horrific concentration camps, filled with thousands of slaves starved to death in the rocket factories.

The allies found much more, something just as horrifying as mass murder. Beneath the picturesque Bavarian town was a labyrinth of tunnels and underground chambers where rockets were constructed and tested. The facility had been built to replace the testing grounds in Peenemunde, the previous production area on the Baltic when it was threatened with being overrun by the Russians.

Major William Castille had spent the better part of the week exploring what he described as a magician's cave. He'd never seen anything like it in his life, the human cruelty displayed here at what must have been a hell for the slaves forced to work here, would stay with him the rest of his life, but it was what he found deep in the tunnels bowels that truly haunted him.

Major Castille was a member of the Army's intelligence unit and had spent the last 72 hours climbing over and crawling through the facility. He just finished his initial search when he spotted Brigadier General Truman Boudinot, the commanding officer of this operation, coming onto the facility grounds. Castille walked over to the general and snapped a smart salute. The general returned the signal.

"Report Major," General Boudinot ordered.

"Sir, we've completed our initial search of the facility. We've determined it to be secure and free of Nazi booby traps. Our exploration has, well to be quite frank, discovered a shocking number of dead. We estimate the number at well over 3,000."

General Boudinot was the image of a typical G.I. square jaw, high forehead ending in a head covered in crew cut dark hair. He removed his helmet, wiped his face with his hand, obviously distressed to hear the news. "Go on Major."

"Sir, we discovered several rocket production lines in various states of destruction. It's obvious; the Nazi's tried to destroy as much as they could before we arrived. However, it appears recent allied bombings prevented the Nazi's from destroying everything. We secured several rockets and rocket components that appear to be in near perfect condition," Major Castille said.

"That's great news, Major. I know the high command is anxious to secure as much Nazi rocket technology as possible. You've done your country a great service," the general stated.

Castille hesitated, as if unsure how to proceed. "You have something more to report Major?" the general asked.

"Ah," Castille stammered. "I think it would be better if I showed you. Please follow me sir."

Castille turned around and headed toward a concrete hangar, the general followed close behind. The two entered the massive facility. The room was littered with abandoned rocket parts, jet fuel tanks, pipes, and building materials. Nazi flags hung on several walls, with a picture of Hitler and Werner Von Bran over the main doorway. The hanger's roof housed a large yellow crane used for moving and lifting rocket parts along the production line. Castille imagined the hangar was a deafening and deadly place when in full operation.

The two continued across the production line toward a set of double doors on the far wall. An elevator call button was on the right. It had been encased in a locked steel case. The case was now little more than twisted metal and rubble.

"This sir is a secure elevator which accesses a testing facility deep below where we currently stand. The army engineers blew up the lock box as you can see, granting access to the lift. Apparently, only a select few had access to the facility below."

Castille pushed the call button and the elevator doors parted almost immediately. The two men entered and turned to face the front of the car. The doors closed behind them. Castille pushed the only button on a small control panel. The car immediately began its descent.

"It's roughly a 30 second ride to the bottom sir," Castille informed his superior.

The ride down was slow and bumpy, yet the elevator car finally came to a halt with a slight thump. The doors parted revealing a long, dark, dank corridor. A string of small naked light bulbs hung from the ceiling, providing just enough illumination to navigate the tunnel.

"Right this way Sir," Castille said indicating the direction with a wave of his open hand. "What I need to show you is just down here."

General Boudinot followed the major down the hallway. The two men walked down the passage in silence coming to a stop at a doorway guarded by two soldiers.

"In here Sir," Castille again said.

The two entered a large room. Castille estimated it to be the size of a basketball court with high ceilings and open floor space. In the room's center was a black triangle shaped craft. The vehicle was ringed by monitors and read out displays. Gauges with German words for pressure, fuel, oxygen printed on them dotted the walls. Hoses and wires criss crossed the floor and connected with the craft at various locations.

"We believe this to be a testing facility of the Nazi's most advanced vehicles including air …" Castille paused considering how best to put it. "and space craft."

"Space craft?" the general asked. "What are you talking about?"

Castille walked over to the black triangle craft. "We've believe this to be the most advanced craft on the planet. My research team has done an initial assessment, very preliminary I must admit, but we are convinced this craft is decades beyond anything the allies have to date."

"What?" General Boudinot asked, his eyes wide with surprise.

"However, that's not the most astonishing finding," Castille hinted. "I've one more thing to show you. You may also want to sit down."

"What are talking about?" the general growled. "I've just fought my way across half of Germany. Hell I nearly walked across a sea of bodies to get to this facility. I think I can handle anything you are about to tell me."

"Okay," Castille said like a man who was about to jump off a high dive into a pool of water of unknown depth. "My men believe this craft is of alien origin."

"Alien? Like Russian or Japanese?" the General questioned.

"No, like not of this world, sir."

"Seriously, and what makes you believe that?"

"Please take a look at this," Castille said pointing at a tube shaped container. It was the size of a mid-sized truck. Castille touched an illuminated button on the container's lid. The lid hissed as a blast of pressurized cold air escaped from its interior. The lid popped up and slid aside on invisible hinges, revealing a coffin like compartment. "Because we found these with the craft."

General Boudinot peered into the compartment, there he saw three very tall, pale creatures. "These aren't human," Boudinot stammered.

"No they aren't," Castille confirmed. "We believe them to be the pilots and crew of the craft over there."

Boudinot alternated his gaze between the creatures and the space craft.

"What's more," Castille started making sure he had Boudinot's full attention. "They are in suspended animation."

"Suspended animation? What the hell is that?"

"They're sleeping. In other words, they're alive."

"Jesus Christ!" Boudinot cussed.

"What should we do with the craft and the aliens sir?" Castille asked, finally getting to the point of the matter.

"I don't know," Boudinot said staring once more into the tube which held the three alien bodies. "This is well above my pay grade; I'll need to talk to President Truman immediately."

Now, here's a special preview of the next
book in

Sean Smith's

Grayson Cole Thriller Series

# Friends like These

The riveting follow up to

## Need to Know

## Lost Cause

and

## Unleashing Colter's Hell

## Prologue

## August 4th, Glacier National Park, MT Eastern border adjacent to the Blackfeet Reservation

The fire was hot, extremely hot. Grayson
Cole felt continually heat waves pulse from

the flame wall that towered above him. The wildfire had reached the forest crown and raced through the tree tops. The fire roared through the forest canopy like a dragon from a fantasy novel cutting through an army of orcs or trolls.

The ponderosa trees that dominated the eastern slopes of the Glacier didn't stand a chance. Glacier's eastern forests were strong. A drought had gripped this part of Montana for years and the forest was dry as chalk. Along with the drought, years of fire suppression had built up western forests like the one of eastern Glacier into a proverbial tinder box. One stray spark, one careless tossed cigarette, one lightning strike would set the forest aflame.

Yet, it wasn't a stray spark or any other innocent cause that started this fire. No, this fire wasn't an act of God, nor a mistake. No, this fire was deliberately set. It was set to achieve a purpose. Its purpose of course was to destroy but more importantly to preserve. The fire would destroy thousands of acres of forest land, pollute countless streams, and blacken the sky. The forest, the streams, the sky would heal in time. In a few years, one wouldn't even know there had been a fire in this part of the park, but something was destroyed that would take decades to recover, if ever. Through its destruction, the arsonist would preserve a way of life, a way of business would continue.

But Grayson Cole knew none of this now. He didn't know the fire was set, nor did he know the fire was set to destroy more than a national park forest. All Park Ranger Grayson Cole cared about right now was the out of control raging fire that was likely to burn another thousand acres before the sunset.

"Jacobs!" Grayson yelled trying to be heard above the roar of the fire.

"Yes, sir?" came the response from a 20 something seasonal firefighter.

"Get on the radio, and tell command we need an eggbeater water dump ASAP!" Cole hollered cupping his hands around his mouth in a futile effort to amplify his voice.

An eggbeater was the slang wildfire fighters used when referring to large type 1 helicopters. The type 1 was one of the big boys capable of dumping the equivalent of a backyard pool's worth of water just about anywhere the firefighter brass wanted.

Jacobs nodded his head in understanding and immediately got on the radio to Park Service air traffic control. Cole knew the helicopter would be on route in a matter of seconds but would it get here in time.

Cole and his team of eight wildfire hot shots had been cutting a line around what was called the "Basin Fire." The fire was so named because of its proximity to the mountain of the same name. The Basin Fire was the park's 32nd fire of the season, putting it on pace for a record fire season. The Basin Fire was shaping up to be one of Glacier's worst in recorded history.

Park firefighting resources, including fire fighters, were stretched thin. Crews from all over the country and even a few foreign ones, had been called in to help. It really didn't make any difference.

Cole knew that some crown fires were so catastrophic that there was little humans and their advanced machinery could do to stop them. Having fought several fires, Cole had come to believe that once a fire reached a certain size it developed what could only be described as a will of its own. He'd seen fire that he'd swear knew what it wanted and where it needed to go. Humans with their puny shovels, axes, even modern helicopters and airplanes, if confronted by such a fire, could do little to dissuade the fire from its intended target.

The Basin Fire was shaping up to be a record breaker. Official park fire records showed that this part of the park had not experienced a fire for more than a century. The forest floor was littered with a hundred years of downed trees, broken branches, and dry needles. Throw in a several year's drought and the Basin area was prime for a fire. And what a fire it was.

The first smoke in the area was reported just 3 days prior. The weather had been mostly clear in the day's preceding with no lightning strikes reported in the area. At first, Park Service management thought they had the resources, including Native American fire crews from the neighboring Blackfeet tribe, but sudden winds had blown what had been a few acre mop up blaze into a monster the size of a small town in little more than 72 hours.

"Thompson, you've got to cut that line to the mineral soil!" Cole yelled at another of his firefighters. "We can't have it jumping our line!"

"Got it boss!" came the reply. Thompson, just like Jacobs, was a 20 something kid. There were one or two 30 somethings on the team, but by that age you were considered a veteran. To be a forty something park superintendent on the fire line was practically unheard of. The other hot shots had taken to calling Cole "Na-akhs", the Blackfoot word for grandfather.

Cole took the good natured ribbing of his hotshots in stride. He knew his heart and mind were willing, but his body had other ideas. The back breaking work of "cutting line" was something more easily done by the kids he was supervising.

Seasonal firefighting was dangerous, hot, dirty, and exhausting work. It wasn't the glamorous stuff shown on TV or in the movies. Cole's face was caked with soot and his eyes burned from the fire's smoke despite a thick pair of goggles.

"Jones! Your fire shelter is coming off your belt," Cole yelled to one of his Blackfeet hotshots. "Secure it!"

The young, dark skinned, Native American from just up the road in Babb Montana, nodded at his boss and did as commanded.

The fire shelter was one of the wildland firefighters most important pieces of equipment and one they never hoped to use. Little more than a Mylar blanket, the fire shelter was a last line of defense for a firefighter if overrun by a blaze. The concept called for firefighters to shelter under the blanket, which protects fire fighters by shielding them from searing heat. The fire fighters called them the "shake and bakes" because once inside one resembled a tin foil wrapped baked potato, that couldn't protect a person from direct flame. The fire shelter would only resist flame, but it too would burn if exposed long enough.

Cole signaled his second in command to join him up on the line. Sinopa Barnes was a 31 year-old Blackfoot firefighter. She bounded up the trail toward her boss with a grace that reminded Cole of a deer, but Barnes was a tough as nails fire fighter. She was a ten year veteran and had fought fires across the continent. She was skilled at cutting line and leading her crews. She could hike and carry equipment with the strongest of men. On this fight however it was her skill with a chain saw that made her most valuable.

Cole saw that Barnes too was coated in soot, her dark skin made even darker by the smears of fire ash across her nose and checks. Her dark eyes were shielded behind her fire goggles. A long braided pony tail of ebony hair hung out from under her blond colored fire helmet. Her yellow nomex shirt and green army fatigues showed the signs of countless fire fights.

"What is it Na-akhs?" Barnes asked.

"Look at this," Cole said pointing at a topographic map of the area. He spread it across a large boulder that served as his make shift table.

"This is where we are," Cole indicated a spot on the map near a green line that marked the border between the park and the Blackfeet reservation. "We are a mere quarter mile from the edge of the park."

Barnes watched closely as Cole explained their current situation.

"Behind us," Cole pointed toward the east in the direction of the reservation. "There is nothing but mixed forest and prairie. Beyond that is the reservation. Thankfully there are few residences in the area and everyone has been evacuated down toward East Glacier while the current fire rages."

Barnes nodded her head and asked "What about the "Praise for the Parks" celebration that was set for East Glacier? Has the event been cancelled?"

"Praise for the Parks" was the annual celebration of the Park Defense Fund. PDF, as it was known nationally, included some of the country's heavyweights including captains of industry, fortune 500 business leaders, presidents of universities, former Secretaries of the Interior, and more than 700,000 dues paying members from every state in the Union. In Washington D.C., PDF was one of the Green Group, the so-called official association of the world's largest environmental groups. The leaders of the various Green Groups commanded six figure salaries and hob-knobbed with the country's elite including A-list celebrities.

"Praise for the Parks" was PDF's opportunity to highlight its accomplishments for the last year, provide a sneak peek of the upcoming year including its political agenda and most importantly squeeze the celebration's select attendees for six, seven, and even eight figure checks. Every year Praise broke fund-raising records and this year was expected to be no different. The fire would put a big crimp in the proceedings.

"Yes, the celebration had to be postponed," Cole said with a slight tinge of sarcasm accenting his use of the word celebration.

"You don't approve of Praise?" Barnes asked.

"Let's just say I think PDF's priorities could benefit from a readjustment," Cole offered. "Anyway, we've got a bigger problem. See this spot here?" Cole pointed to a hand drawn X on his map that straddled the park and reservation border.

"That's InGenetics," Barnes said. "I know it well. It's a genetic research company run by Dr. George Running Wolf, the Blackfeet chief. "Rumor has it his company found a cure for Alzheimer's. They are just waiting for FDA approval. It's the talk of the entire reservation and could mean huge economic benefits for our little part of the world."

"That's right," Cole agreed. What Barnes said was right; InGenetics represented a huge opportunity for the Blackfeet Nation. However, what she didn't mention was the lab's construction and operation was highly controversial. The company, citing Native American treaties, was permitted to partially construct their facility on park service land. That wasn't the controversial part, no InGenetics actually secured permission to "harvest" a select number of the park's grizzly bears for its research. Biological studies have found that bears lose up to 30 percent of their brain function while hibernating. However, when spring hits brain function returns with little or no loss of memory. InGenetics scientists harvested several bears to study their brains and determine the reason for restored brain function.

The problem, as some saw it, was that the Glacier Grizzly Bear population was dangerously small without bears being taken for research. Any bear killed, especially females, had a significant impact upon the species long-term survival. Moreover, federal law at the time, prevented the Park Service from making a profit on the sale of park resources, therefore the agency most responsible for protecting this vulnerable species stood to gain nothing from the discovery. In other words, the American public foots the bill for the animals' protection, while a private company gains the profit from its exploitation.

This fact struck several as unfair, illegal, and immoral. Most notably the Bear Field Defenders or BFD, as they were more commonly known, objected to the exploitation even before it was officially announced. BFD was a direct action, no-holds barred, San Francisco based group of what most saw as throw back hippies and tree huggers. They were seen as unwashed, granola eating, Birkenstock wearing socialists. Those who followed BFD closely also knew the group was adept at filing rule making petitions, information requests, and legal challenges which could keep the park service tied up in legal knots for years. Yet, BFD wasn't above bending, some claimed breaking, the rules. Their opposition to the InGenetics lab had become the stuff of legend. Once the park service approved the permit for the harvest of five bears by InGenetics hired sharpshooters, BFD activists and volunteers spent the entirety of several summers in the parks making noise, hiking in large groups, and generally harassing both the hunters and any potential bears in the area. After several failed hunting seasons, InGenetics filed a court case with the Montana district court in the hopes of securing an injunction against BFD. The court threw it out, citing the groups right to free speech. InGenetics changed tactics after that, securing a permit to lure bears out of the park and onto the Blackfeet reservation. Once on the reservation, the tribe gave InGenetics, with Park Service approval, the authorization to shoot the bears. The Blackfeet charged BFD members who ventured onto the reservation in pursuit of the bears, with trespass, saddling them with hefty fines.

BFD changed tactics as well, taking to the air in rented fixed wing aircraft and helicopters in an attempt at continuing the harassment. All BFD's efforts eventually failed, as InGenetics merely moved the hunts to nightfall obscuring the actually killing of the bears under the cover of darkness.

After that, BFD's park operations ended and the organization turned to direct action. They boycotted InGenetics stockholder meetings in San Francisco, by dressing like corporate bigwigs and smearing fake blood on their hands. They picketed outside key stockholders houses, writing on their streets in large letters "BFD" and "Smokey Bear Killers live here!" The media ate it up. Eventually all the noise and effort failed. InGenetics built its lab and got its bears.

BFD's activists faded away and for the past three years InGenetics had been harvesting 5 bears every year. Rumors out of the lab indicated that InGenetics Alzheimer efforts had found a cure - that was the good news. The downside, in order to scale up the serum, it would require a large and steady supply of bears. InGenetics expected announcement would, to many in the BFD community, signal the end of America's wild Grizzly bear population.

Cole tapped the map's red X which indicated InGenetics' location, "And it's about the only structure out here. And given we are the only fire crew in the area, it's our job to make sure this fire doesn't reach that building."

Cole knew firefighting 101 required fire crews to prioritize its efforts to first protect human life, second protect structures, and third other resources like forests and meadows. Since there weren't any people in the area, Cole's primary goal was to protect the InGenetics lab. Even if it wasn't his top priority from a firefighting standpoint, Cole was savvy enough to know that protecting InGenetics was good strategy from a political standpoint. As Barnes had pointed out, the lab had the potential to be a billion dollar infusion into the Blackfeet Nation. Letting a billion dollar golden goose burn to the ground would be a tough thing to explain to a congressional committee Cole knew. As such, he couldn't let it happen.

"Here's what we are going to do," Cole started speaking to Barnes. "I want you, Jones, and Sanchez to begin clearing a line from here," Cole pointed at a spot on the map, "to here. Make sure the line is at least 3 feet wide, we can't afford to have the fire get behind us. Understand?"

Barnes nodded her understanding.

"Good, the eggbeaters should be on scene shortly, but we can't rely on them to snuff out this fire. We are going to have to do it, at least this portion on our own. Got it?"

Again, Barnes nodded her head.

"Get going then," Cole said, excusing the 30 something firefighter to her work.

Cole and the remaining hotshots fell in behind Barnes and her team. The ten person crew looked like a modern train track crew. The team swung its axes, pickaxes, and pulsakis in rhythm with each other. Like a twenty armed forest clearing monster, the team set an impressive pace through the woods.

Occasionally, the rotors of an "egg beater" could be heard through the roar of the fire and the team adjusted its pace to accommodate the helicopter's pending water dump. Hour after hour the team cut line.

Around 3 in the afternoon, Cole paused to assess his team. He was pushing them, but they were all young and in good shape. He knew they could handle it. Cole grabbed his water bottle from his belt and drank down a large slug of water. He was sweating profusely and it took all the water he was carrying to stay hydrated.

He placed the cap back on the bottle. As he screwed down the lid, a small piece of ash flitted about and landed softly on his gloved hand.

*Odd*, Cole thought as the feather like piece of burnt wood had come from behind him. The fire he was fighting laying directly in front with the wind at his back. Ash from this fire shouldn't be coming from behind him.

Cole slowly turned around to reveal the InGenetics lab and forest that ringed the complex like a blanket, fully engulfed in flame.

"Shit! Barnes, we've got a problem!" Cole yelled to his lieutenant. The scene of the lab fully engulfed in flame, belching black smoke into the air took Cole by surprise. His team had been meticulous to chase down every stray ember, every flit of flame was stamped out. Nothing had gotten behind them. That building should not be on fire. But it surely was.

Barnes was sprinting her way back to her boss, obviously fully aware of the trap the team was in.

"Barnes we've got a bit of a situation here," Cole started. "Get on the radio and update the egg beaters to our situation. Tell them we are going to need a water dump, no check that, several water dumps directly on our location."

Barnes frantically nodded. "Yes, boss."

Cole turned his attention back to the InGenetics fire. It was growing quickly already engulfing the surrounding forest but now helped by the wind, moving up the slight incline toward Cole's team. He realized the fire would overrun his team's position soon.

Cole waved his arms above his head to get his hotshot's attention. All stopped what they were doing and turned toward their boss.

"The fire behind us has cut off the escape route to our safe area," Cole began. He scanned around looking for another place to shelter from the all but certain burn over facing his team.

Uphill and slightly to their right was a small outcropping of rock. If his team squeezed in tight, all ten just might be able to deploy their "shake and bakes" and ride out the flames. *Might*. It was a low probability of success option, but it was their only option. Cole wasn't going to tell his team that though.

"Let's head to those rocks," Cole yelled pointing to the collection of car sized boulders. "Barnes? What's the word on the helicopter?"

Barnes ran up to join the rest of the team, it's on its way but it will likely be five minutes until they can get a water dump on our position."

*Five minutes? The fire will be on us well before then,* Cole thought. "Okay, tell the team to get in their fire shelters and hunker down. It could get really hot in a few seconds."

Barnes set off to carry out her boss's orders. Cole turned back to see the InGenetic's fire had now fully engulfed the surrounding forest, it jumped into the forest canopy sending red hot flames dozens of feet into the air above the already hundred foot trees.

Cole didn't believe in Hell or the Devil, but if he did he imagined Lucifer might look like a hundred foot wall of flames that was barreling down on his team. He could see that the fire would overrun them in a matter of seconds. It was time for him to get into his own "shake and bake."

Cole sprinted the basketball court distance to the makeshift "safety zone", his hotshots were already in their shelters looking like ten human sized aluminum wrapped hotdogs. *This is not going to be pretty,* Cole thought.

314

The flame wall was only a few feet away now. Thick smoke overwhelmed the team's position like the leading clouds of a building hurricane. *If the fire doesn't kill us, the smoke surely will,* Cole knew. Coles eyes and nose burned due to the acrid smoke. It contained a slight chemical scent, which Cole thought odd. Not your typical fire smoke smell. The heat was getting unbearable. Even through his heat resistant nomex clothes, heavy gloves, and thick gloves every part of his body could feel the temperature rise. He imagined this is what it was like to be a potato in an oven. At least it's a dry heat he joked with himself

Cole could hear the grunts and coughs of his teammates, the temperature and smoke was growing unbearable. "Hold on everyone," Cole choked out. "Stay put, the helicopter will be here shortly." What he didn't know was if the helicopter would be there in time.

The roar of the fire and the howl of the wind began to build to a deafening level. It would soon be nearly impossible to communicate or even hear his team. Perhaps it was for the better, he dreaded hearing the screams of his team burning alive. He hoped death would come quickly, but feared it might not. He could already feel the hair on his head and arms starting to singe, small wisps of smoke rising from every follicle.

Through the roar, just on the edge of being audible, Cole thought he could make out the beat of a drum. *Who would be playing instruments during a fire storm?* Cole thought. The drumming continued to grow. *I must be losing my mind or perhaps it's the pulse of my own blood? Maybe this is what happens to people who are burned alive.*

The drum beat continued to grow louder and more steady. It was as if the drummer was right on top of them.

"BOSS!" Barnes yelled her voice nearly drowned out by the fire and the drumming. "The helicopters are here! They are directly over us and want to know where to dump their water!"

"Tell them to drop it right on top of us! NOW!"

Cole could hear Barnes screaming to the pilot's to drop the water on their current position. It was a risk Cole knew, if they missed hitting the right spot the fire would continue to burn right over them. If the drop was too low it could knock loose the hotshots' grip on their fire shelters and leave them vulnerable to being burned. Dropped to high, the water would dissipate before it even hit the ground, again leaving them to be roasted alive.

It would have to be a perfect shot.

Cole could now hear and feel the helicopters directly over his position. The rotor noise was deafening, while the rotor prop wash was making it nearly impossible to hold onto his fire shelter. The rotor gusts had the benefit of keeping the flames at bay, at least for the moment.

Cole heard the mechanical click of the helicopter's water bucket opening its chute and a cascade of more than 2000 gallons of water cascaded out of it. The water hit the team like a wave crashing onto a beach. The team was washed from the protected perch and scattered around the base of the rock outcropping.

Cole lost hold of his fire shelter; the crashing water ripped it from his grip. The torrent of water tumbled him head over heels. When he finally came to a stop, he was resting on his back a dozen yards from where he'd began.

His firefighting crew was similarly spread across the base of the rock outcropping, all were soaked but at quick glance all appeared okay.

Cole looked up to see the second helicopter dropping its water load a few yards from his team's current position. The pilot was obviously creating an escape route through the burning forest to a safer area for the trapped firefighters.

"Move!" Cole commanded the now dirty and drenched young men and women. Everyone did as their boss commanded. The team sprinted through the helicopter created path, but Cole knew it wouldn't last long. They would have to reach a previously burned over area to escape the flames. Leaving their fire shelters behind, there would be no plan B if they didn't make it to safety.

Up ahead Cole could see the fire beginning to reclaim the forest, only temporarily squelched by the helicopter's dump of lake water. Like the scene from the Ten Commandments where the Red Sea drowns the Egyptian's in pursuit of the fleeing Israelites, the forest fire began to close in on the fleeing crew from both sides.

Above a small rise, Cole spotted what he'd been looking for, a previously charred area of the forest. His team could retreat and hunker there, safe, knowing that everything that could burn had already been consumed by the fire. "There!" Cole yelled pointing at the black area which just the day before had been a meadow overgrown with wildflowers.

Their safety zone would still be unbearably hot, but at least they could escape the flames and much of the smoke. The team would survive.

The team broke into a full sprint now, Cole brought up the rear. One by one his ten teammates made it to safety. Cole was just feet behind them. The fire continued to close in, like the walls of a trash compacter. Fire lit the sleeve of Cole's shirt. He damped it out with his gloved hand while continuing his sprint. *This is going to be close,* he thought.

He was a mere ten feet from the finish when a wave of fire poured over his path. Without hesitation Cole barreled through the wall of fire, diving the last few feet to safety. He must have looked like a baserunner sliding into home base in a ball game played in Hell. He'd cleared the flames and came to a screeching halt at the feet of his already assembled crew. From the looks on their faces, he could tell they didn't think he would have made it.

Cole scrambled to his feet, "Everyone okay?"

They nodded their heads, obviously just now taking in the gravity of what they had just been through.

"Good, try and hunker down. Get some shelter from the heat. We may be here a while!" Cole ordered. Everyone did as commanded. There was no need to tell anyone twice.

Cole followed the team, but stopped to take a quick look back at where they had been. The forest was once again fully engulfed in flames. The spot where they had previously taken refuge from the fire was now fully consumed as well. Cole could just make out through the smoke and flame a few of the fire shelters melting in the heat. He knew everyone would be dead if they had stayed put.

Cole wiped his eyes, they stung from the heavy smoke in the air. Through a break in the haze he could see the InGenetics lab had been reduced to a pile of smoldering rubble. At that moment, he knew that there would be no Alzheimer cure in the near future.

Somebody just lost a ton of money, Cole knew. What the ranger didn't know is that at that very moment, somebody else stood to make a great deal more.

## ABOUT THE AUTHOR

Sean Smith is an award winning conservationist and author, whose work has been seen on CNN, heard on NPR, and covered in the New York Times and National Geographic.

Sean is a former park ranger who worked at Yellowstone, the North Cascades, Glacier national parks, and with the Forest Service at Mount St. Helens. He's also an accomplished artist, as well as a private pilot.

Recently, Sean began writing political thrillers

set in National Parks. His goal is to entertain his readers, but also educate them on the challenges park rangers face every day while protecting America's heritage.

He currently lives in Western Washington with his wife and two children.

- Contact Sean at: seanwrites@yahoo.com

- Or visit: SeanDavidSmith.blogspot.com

- Like him on Facebook, www.facebook.com/parkthrillers

- Or follow him on Twitter: @parkthrillers

Made in the USA
Monee, IL
14 September 2020

42442356R00177